From the BookFest 2026 3rd Place–Winning Romance Series

She Came at the Glass Heel
Book 3

Neon Diner

Tatiana Vixen Reyes

For transgender women who took a
seat and found something they didn't
know they were looking for.

Chapter 1

Becoming Lily

The night air bit at Lily's cheeks like tiny glass teeth as she took her place in the line outside The Glass Heel, where the neon sign flickered crimson against the black sky, casting everyone in a pulsing, otherworldly glow. Her third visit, and still the flutter in her stomach hadn't subsided. If anything, it had intensified—the knowledge of what waited beyond those heavy mahogany doors made anticipation curl through her veins like smoke from the cigarettes being passed between strangers ahead of her.

She exhaled, watching her breath bloom white in the January darkness, dissipating into the starless Chicago night. The click of her silver stiletto heels against the icy pavement had felt confident in the warm sanctuary of her apartment; now each step seemed to announce her presence too loudly on the frozen concrete. I'm here. I'm back. I'm still not sure I belong.

The line ahead shuffled forward, a caterpillar of humanity inching toward warmth. Bodies huddled against the cold, leather jackets pressed against sequined tops, conversations drifting in fragmented whispers that formed temporary clouds between painted lips. Lily tugged her gossamer wrap tighter around her bare shoulders, the emerald silk offering little protection against the wind that sliced between steel-and-glass buildings and found every exposed inch of her goosebumped skin. She'd chosen the shimmering dress with its dangerously low back for the woman she wanted to be tonight, not for practicality in a Chicago winter that transformed each breath into a visible confession.

"You're shivering," said a voice behind her.

Lily turned, startled by the proximity. The woman smiled, a flash of perfect white teeth in the dark, her face half-illuminated by the neon sign that pulsed above the entrance. The crimson light caught the sharp angle of her cheekbone, then slid away into shadow, revealing and concealing her features in hypnotic rhythm. Her eyes—dark and knowing beneath precisely arched brows—remained fixed on Lily's face with an intensity that felt like recognition, though they'd never met.

"First time?" the woman asked.

"Third," Lily admitted, surprising herself with the honesty. "Still feels like the first, though."

The woman laughed, the sound warm against the cold. "That feeling never quite goes away. That's the magic of this place."

The line moved again, bodies shifting forward in unison. Lily could see Darius at the door now, his broad shoulders stretching the seams of his black fitted jacket, the silver earpiece wire curling behind his ear catching the crimson neon as he checked IDs with the efficient grace of a dancer. Her pulse quickened, fluttering beneath the thin skin of her throat. Three visits didn't make her a regular—not like the woman ahead who exchanged a familiar nod with him—but it meant something. A commitment, perhaps. An admission that whatever she'd found inside those walls was worth braving the Chicago winter that turned her breath to fog and numbed her fingertips, worth the risk of being seen by someone who might recognize her Monday-through-Friday self.

The bass from inside thumped faintly against the pavement beneath her stilettos, vibrating up through the soles of her feet like a heartbeat calling her forward. Lily straightened her spine, feeling the cool air against the exposed skin of her back, and took another step toward the door, toward the version of herself—wilder, braver, unnamed—that existed only within The Glass Heel's velvet-draped embrace.

When Lily reached the entrance, Darius's eyes met hers—amber-flecked irises that missed nothing beneath heavy lids. Six-foot-four of quiet authority, he stood like a sentinel against the night, his obsidian skin catching the crimson neon glow that traced the sculpted edges of his cheekbones. The silver hoop in his left ear winked with each subtle movement of his head, and his massive hands—capable of both gentleness and swift removal of trouble—rested loosely at his sides, ready.

"Evening," he said, his deep voice carrying just enough warmth to cut through the chill. He extended his hand for her ID, though Lily sensed it was more formality than necessity.

"Hi, Darius." His name felt new on her tongue, an

intimacy she was still getting used to. She fumbled in her clutch, fingers stiff with cold as she extracted her driver's license.

He examined it briefly, the ghost of a smile touching his lips. "Ms. Warren. Third time's the charm."

Lily blinked in surprise. "You remember?"

"It's my job to notice patterns." He handed back her ID, then stepped slightly aside to clear her path. "You're becoming a familiar face."

Something loosened in Lily's chest—a knot of twisted silk ribbons she hadn't realized was there until it began to unravel, thread by gossamer thread. Not quite belonging yet, but no longer a complete stranger either. She occupied some middle ground that felt like standing in the shallows of a midnight ocean—the sand still solid beneath her feet, but each gentle wave washing away her footprints, erasing the evidence of her hesitation while leaving her essence intact.

"The cold didn't keep you away," he observed, his gaze taking in her inadequate wrap with professional assessment.

"Some things are worth the frostbite," she replied, surprising herself with the quip.

Darius's laugh was brief but genuine. "Echo will be pleased to hear it." He nodded toward the inner door. "Enjoy your evening, Ms. Warren. Marisol's at coat check tonight."

As Lily stepped past him into the lobby's welcoming warmth, she felt the weight of his presence behind her—not threatening but protective, like crossing a threshold under a guardian's watch. The amber sconces along the cherrywood-paneled walls cast the space in honeyed light, and the music from beyond the velvet curtains beckoned with a muffled pulse.

Lily drew closer to the photographs, mesmerized by the history captured in each frame. A grand opening gala from June 1993 showed Echo—looking impossibly young yet somehow ageless—cutting a ribbon across the entrance. In another, drag performers with towering wigs and sequined gowns posed before a packed house. The images progressed through the decades: protest signs and rainbow flags from the early 2000s; a candlelit vigil; celebrities whose faces she recognized mingling with club regulars; and more recent shots showing the evolution of the space into what it had become today.

"We're all just chapters in a very long story," came a lilting voice from behind the coat check counter.

Lily turned to find Marisol watching her, their obsidian curls cascading over one shoulder like spilled ink against bronze skin. Their eyes—bright with mischief and rimmed with a perfect wing of copper liner—caught the amber light from above. Tonight they wore a high-necked cream blouse from another era, its silk organza sleeves billowing from tightly-cuffed wrists as they gestured toward the wall of photographs with fingers adorned in an assortment of vintage silver rings.

"Some nights I wonder which of us will end up framed on that wall," Marisol said, leaning forward on their elbows. Their gaze swept over Lily's dress, and their painted lips curved into an appreciative smile. "Well, look at you, stepping up your game. That dress is giving me everything I need tonight."

Heat crept up Lily's neck. "I, um... thank you." She fumbled with the silk wrap, suddenly self-conscious under Marisol's appraising eye.

"Let me take that before you strangle yourself with it," Marisol teased, reaching across the counter. Their fingers brushed Lily's as they took the wrap, and Lily caught a whiff of something spicy and warm—cinnamon, maybe, or clove. "You won't be needing this inside. Trust me, it gets plenty hot once the night really starts."

Lily's fingers slipped from the silk as Marisol took it, their hands briefly touching. The wrap billowed like water before Marisol captured it with a flick of the wrist, draping it over a polished wooden hanger in one fluid motion. The brass hook clinked against the rail as they turned, eyes finding Lily's again, lips curved into that same knowing smile.

"Third time's a pattern, you know," Marisol said, their voice dropping to a conspiratorial whisper. "Two visits might be coincidence, but three? That's commitment. You're becoming one of us."

They slid a brass token across the polished mahogany counter, its weight substantial against Lily's palm. The club's signature stiletto heel was embossed deep into the metal, worn smooth at the edges from countless nights of safekeeping. Marisol's fingers—adorned with those vintage silver rings that caught the amber light—lingered over Lily's for a heartbeat longer than necessary, warm and slightly rough at the fingertips, like someone who worked with their hands despite their elegant appearance.

"Keep this safe. It's not just for your coat—it's your key to coming back."

When Lily looked up, Marisol's eyes—dark as espresso with flecks of amber catching the low light—held hers with unexpected gentleness. The slight softening at the corners, the barely perceptible tilt of their head, spoke a language Lily hadn't realized she understood until this moment. Something shifted in her chest, like a door long-rusted suddenly swinging open on silent hinges. The air between them seemed to thicken and warm, carrying Marisol's silent message across the polished mahogany: You belong here. Not merely tolerated, but welcomed. Expected, even, like the final piece of a puzzle they'd been waiting to complete.

"Go on in," Marisol said, nodding toward the velvet curtains. "Julian's working the bar tonight, and Echo's been in a generous mood. The DJ started a new set five minutes ago." Marisol winked. "Don't miss it."

With the token warm in her palm—a small brass sun radiating heat into her skin—Lily took a steadying breath and approached the velvet curtains. They hung heavy and plush, the color of midnight wine, their edges trimmed with gold thread that caught the amber light. She parted them with trembling fingers, feeling the soft resistance against her skin, and stepped through the threshold that separated observer from participant.

The Glass Heel opened before her like a midnight bloom. The air changed instantly—thicker, warmer, electric with possibility. Bass notes vibrated through the soles of her feet, traveling up her legs and settling low in her belly. Lily paused, letting her eyes adjust to the dimness broken only by strategically placed lights that caught the movement of bodies on the dance floor.

Sapphire-upholstered booths lined the perimeter, their high backs offering illusions of privacy. In each one, candles flickered in mercury glass holders, painting faces in golden light that made everyone look like they belonged in a Renaissance painting—all shadow and revelation. The ceiling soared above, unexpected in its height, strung with delicate lights that mimicked stars against midnight blue.

The air was thick with colliding scents: jasmine and

sandalwood perfumes, cedar-based colognes, and the honest salt of bodies in motion, all suspended in the humid warmth like invisible smoke. Each breath filled Lily's lungs with this living perfume, making her head swim pleasantly. Beneath these human notes lingered something more deliberate—dragon's blood incense burning somewhere unseen, its crimson scent threading through the space like a secret whispered directly into her bloodstream.

The music pulsed through the room, a steady beat that seemed to synchronize with her own quickening pulse. Heather's set was a symphony of electronic beats layered with haunting vocals that floated above the crowd like spectral whispers. Bass notes vibrated through the floorboards and up Lily's legs, while crystalline high tones shimmered in the air around her head. The music seemed to swirl around her, filling the room with invisible currents that pulled dancers together and apart like tides.

Bodies moved on the dance floor—a silver-haired woman in her sixties with arms raised skyward, a pair of androgynous twins in matching velvet suits, a tall Black man with vitiligo patterns across his face like beautiful constellations. They danced not with the awkward, self-conscious movements of other clubs Lily had visited, but with an abandon that made her throat tighten. A heavily tattooed woman in a wheelchair spun at the edge of the floor, her head thrown back in laughter as a partner in a flowing silk jumpsuit leaned down to whisper in her ear. Here, dancing wasn't performance but release—as if everyone had checked their daytime selves at the door with their coats.

"First you hover by the door, then you'll circle the perimeter twice before deciding whether to approach the bar," came a voice to her left. "I've been watching your pattern."

Julian stood there, towel slung over one broad shoulder, a knowing smile playing at the corners of his full mouth. The sleeves of his burgundy henley were pushed up to reveal forearms corded with lean muscle and a tattoo of intertwined vines that disappeared beneath the fabric. He wasn't supposed to be away from the bar, Lily thought, but somehow his presence beside her felt right—the warmth radiating from him cutting through the club's sensory overload like a beacon—as if he'd appointed himself her temporary guide through this labyrinth of sound and sensation.

"I don't have a pattern," she protested, but the heat in her cheeks betrayed her.

"Three visits is enough data to establish one." His voice carried just enough over the music without shouting. "Come on, I'll walk you to the bar. Save you fifteen minutes of indecision."

Lily trailed Julian through the crowd. Bodies made way for him—not out of respect, but with that instinctive acknowledgment animals give to larger creatures. She quickened her pace to stay in the path he carved. Ahead, the bar materialized through the haze of moving bodies—a long concrete slab where crushed mirror shards caught light like constellations frozen in stone. Behind it, bottles climbed the wall in a spectrum of colors: honey-amber whiskeys, clear crystalline vodkas, deep blue gins. One corner housed jewel-colored non-alcoholic options. A brass ladder, that supposedly once belonged to Chicago's library, slid along rails beside these liquid treasures. The whole arrangement commanded attention like some temple to intoxication, both practical and sacred.

"What'll it be tonight?" Julian asked as he slipped

behind the bar. "Your usual vodka soda with a whisper of lime, or are you ready to try something new?" His dark eyes held a challenge, the corner of his mouth quirking upward.

Lily leaned against the smooth wood of the bar, her heartbeat quickening. "What makes you think I need something new?"

"Third visit." Julian reached for a glass, his movements fluid and precise. "Third visits are for shedding skin. First time, you're just seeing if you can walk through the door. Second, you're testing if the first time was a fluke." His voice dropped slightly. "Third time? That's when you start becoming who you really are."

Behind him, Miko moved with quiet efficiency, preparing three drinks at once without seeming rushed. Her dark bob swung forward as she leaned to grab a bottle from a lower shelf, the line of her neck elegant in the diffused light. She glanced up, meeting Lily's eyes for a brief moment before returning to her work, but that fleeting connection felt like permission.

"Alright," Lily conceded, squaring her shoulders slightly. "What do you recommend?"

Julian's smile widened. "For you? Something that bites back." He reached for a bottle with amber liquid, its label obscured by his deft hands. "Sweet enough to tempt you, strong enough to remind you you're alive."

"That sounds..." Lily hesitated, searching for the word. "Dangerous."

"Only the best things are." Julian's hands moved in a practiced dance, adding bitters, a twist of something citrus, a splash from another bottle. "Danger isn't always about risk. Sometimes it's about revelation."

Miko appeared at Julian's side, sliding a small plate of candied ginger toward Lily. "To complement what he's making you," she explained, her voice measured and calm. "Julian has good instincts, but his palate needs refinement." The subtle curve of her lips took any sting from the words.

Julian placed a tumbler before Lily, the liquid inside catching the light like trapped fire. "Bourbon with notes of caramel and spice, elevated with orange bitters and a touch of amaro. We call it 'Becoming.'"

"Very poetic," Lily murmured, lifting the glass. The aroma hit her first—warm, complex, slightly intimidating. She took a tentative sip and felt the heat bloom across her tongue, followed by layers of flavor that unfolded one after another. The burn was gentler than she expected, transforming into warmth that traveled down her throat and spread through her chest.

"Oh," she breathed, surprised by her own reaction.

"Good 'oh' or overwhelmed 'oh'?" Julian asked, watching her face with genuine interest.

"Good. Definitely good." Lily took another sip, more confident this time. "It tastes like... like autumn and secrets."

Miko's soft laugh caught Lily by surprise. "She has a better palate than you, Julian."

Julian grinned, unfazed by Miko's teasing. "She's a natural."

The crowd shifted suddenly, like a wave receding from shore. Lily noticed it first in the subtle straightening of Julian's posture, then in the way conversations around her softened, creating a strange pocket of anticipation in the room's atmosphere. She turned, following the direction of whispered attention.

Echo Dela Cruz moved through the club like a ship parting water. Her black dress—a liquid silk that clung to her curves before falling away in a dramatic asymmetrical hem—caught the light in ways that seemed to defy physics, simultaneously absorbing and reflecting the glow from overhead. At her throat, a pendant of a miniature glass heel hung from a delicate silver chain, capturing and fracturing the club's lights into tiny rainbows that danced across her collarbones. Silver threads woven through her dress sparked like distant stars with each deliberate step. Her presence commanded the space without effort, her chin tilted at precisely the angle between approachable and regal. Lily found herself holding her breath as Echo paused to touch a shoulder here, her long fingers adorned with a single platinum ring, or exchange words there, her crimson lips barely moving yet somehow perfectly heard despite the music. These brief moments left people looking slightly dazed in her wake, as if they'd been brushed by something rare and dangerous.

"She makes her rounds every night," Julian murmured, leaning closer to Lily. "Checks the pulse of the room."

Lily nodded, unable to look away as Echo approached, her path now unmistakably angled toward the bar. Toward her. Lily's fingers tightened around her glass.

"Julian," Echo's voice carried a warmth that seemed reserved for her staff. "How is the new amaro working out?"

"Like it was made for us," he replied with easy confidence. "Lily here is the first to try the 'Becoming.'"

Echo's silver-gray eyes shifted to Lily, and the full weight of her attention felt like stepping from shadow into spotlight. Lily swallowed hard.

"Lily Warren," Echo said, her crimson lips curving into a smile that seemed to hold secrets. "Third visit in as many weeks. The dress is exquisite on you."

A flush crept up Lily's neck. She hadn't expected Echo to remember her name, let alone keep track of her visits. "Thank you," she managed, her voice steadier than she felt. "The drink is wonderful."

Echo stepped closer, the scent of jasmine and clove enveloping Lily like a spell. "Tell me," she said, her voice dropping to create an intimate space between them despite the crowd, "what brings you back to us?"

The question hung in the air, deceptively simple yet impossibly complex. Lily took another sip of her drink for courage, feeling the warmth spread through her chest.

"I'm not entirely sure," she admitted, surprising herself with her honesty. "Something about this place feels... possible."

Echo's silver-gray eyes held hers for a moment that stretched like warm honey poured from a spoon, the tiny flecks of gold near her pupils catching the light as she searched for something Lily couldn't name. The woman's perfectly arched eyebrow lifted a fraction of an inch, her gaze moving deliberately across Lily's features as if reading a language written there. Whatever she found in that careful inspection seemed to satisfy her, because she nodded once, decisively, the movement causing her obsidian earrings to sway against the elegant column of her neck.

"Possibility is precisely what we cultivate here, Lily." Echo's hand brushed Lily's arm, the touch light but deliberate. "I hope you find what you're looking for, whether you know what that is yet or not."

With that, Echo moved on, leaving behind a void that the club's energy rushed to fill. Lily cradled her drink, the bourbon's warmth spreading through her chest with each sip. When she turned to survey the room, the dance floor had transformed—where there had been space, now bodies undulated to the beat of Heather's newest track. The lights played across skin and metal, catching the glint of earrings, necklaces, and the first dewy sheen of exertion as the night deepened its hold.

She leaned against the bar, one elbow resting on the cool surface that caught the light like trapped fire, and took it all in. The faces of strangers—flushed with alcohol and bathed in indigo light—somehow didn't feel like strangers anymore. A woman with a geometric undercut threw her head back, her laughter rising above the bass line before dissolving into the swirl of conversation. Across the room, a tall figure in a silver mesh top caught the eye of someone at the corner table, their shared glance electric with unspoken invitation. Her third visit, and still The Glass Heel revealed new corners, new mysteries—hidden alcoves where couples disappeared behind velvet curtains, bartenders performing alchemy with bottles she couldn't name, and the whispered conversations that seemed to pulse with the same rhythm as Heather's hypnotic beats.

That's when she saw him.

Across the room, partially hidden by a fluted marble column near the DJ booth, stood a man whose absolute stillness made him magnetic in a room full of frenetic movement. Devon. She hadn't known his name during her previous visits, had only caught fleeting glimpses of him watching the crowd with the same careful, anthropological attention she gave it. Tonight he wore a fitted black shirt with subtle geometric patterns woven into the fabric that caught the light only when he shifted his weight, emphasizing the breadth of his shoulders and the lean strength of his forearms where he'd rolled the sleeves to just below his elbows. The warm umber of his skin caught the cobalt-blue lights in a way that outlined his sharp cheekbones and the strong line of his jaw, making him look otherworldly, like a being who existed half in this reality and half in another.

As if sensing her gaze, Devon's eyes—dark as obsidian but ringed with an unexpected amber—lifted and met hers directly across thirty feet of writhing bodies and spilled drinks. The connection jolted through Lily like an electric current, raising goosebumps along her arms despite the heat of the crowded room. No polite glance away, no pretending the contact hadn't happened. Instead, he held her gaze with unwavering focus, his expression unreadable but intent, one eyebrow lifting a fraction of an inch in what might have been challenge or invitation.

Lily's fingers tightened around her glass until her knuckles blanched white against the crystal. She should look away. Should turn back to the bar, order another drink with a name like a whispered promise, lose herself in conversation with Julian's easy charm or Miko's razor-sharp wit. Instead, she found herself unable to break the tenuous silver thread that stretched between them across the sea of bodies, fragile as spider silk but strong as piano wire.

His full lips curved slightly—not quite a smile, but an acknowledgment that hummed with electricity. Recognition that flickered like the club's indigo lights catching on the single silver ring adorning his left middle finger. As if they'd met before in some other context, some other life where the air wasn't thick with jasmine and bourbon and possibility.

Had they? Lily racked her memory, mentally thumbing through the Rolodex of faces that had crossed her path. A coffee shop with copper tables and mismatched mugs? The 6:15 train where she always stood by the third door? The modern wing of the art museum where she sometimes spent her lunch breaks, losing herself in canvases of violent color? But no, she would have remembered him. The quiet confidence in the way his weight settled into one hip, the steady weight of his obsidian-amber gaze that seemed to see past her carefully selected dress to the woman beneath—these weren't things one forgot, couldn't be misplaced like keys or an umbrella.

Chapter 2

Devon's Ease

The city night folded around Devon like a well-worn jacket as he approached The Glass Heel, its neon sign buzzing electric rich red against the brick facade. January wind cut sharp across his face, slicing through his stubble and numbing the tip of his nose, but he barely registered the cold. Six visits in, and something about this place still pulled at him—a gravity he couldn't quite explain to himself, like a splinter beneath the skin of his consciousness.

The line outside was modest tonight, perhaps twenty bodies huddled against the chill, leather jackets and wool scarves inadequate armor against the biting air. Conversations rose in plumes of white breath that dissipated into the darkness. Devon bypassed the wait with measured steps, his boots crunching on the salt-crusted sidewalk, nodding to a few faces he recognized from previous nights—the woman with the silver septum ring, the tall man with immaculate dreadlocks. Not friends, not yet, but no longer strangers either. The in-between space felt comfortable, like breaking in new shoes that had finally stopped pinching at the heel.

Darius stood sentinel at the entrance, his imposing six-foot-four frame haloed by fractured light pouring from inside—ruby reds and cobalt blues from the club's stained glass windows spilling onto the sidewalk in geometric patterns that transformed his silhouette into something almost ecclesiastical. A gold hoop earring caught a shard of crimson when he turned his head. Their eyes met through this kaleidoscope glow, and Devon felt the familiar assessment—quick, professional, a flicker of recognition in those dark irises. Darius's shoulders relaxed beneath a black Carhartt jacket worn thin at the elbows, its collar faded from sun and sweat, a small tear near the pocket patched with what looked like roofing tape.

"Carter," Darius said, his deep voice carrying just enough warmth to distinguish Devon from the first-timers. "Back again."

"Can't stay away," Devon replied, handing over his ID more out of ritual than necessity. The plastic was cool against his fingers, a small reminder of the world outside these walls.

Darius examined the card briefly before returning it with a subtle nod. "Making a habit of us."

"Trying to," Devon admitted. Something about Darius's steady presence invited honesty, as if the man's solid reliability created a pocket of truth around him.

"Six visits," Darius observed, stepping slightly aside to clear Devon's path. "You're on the edge now."

"The edge?"

"Between visitor and fixture." The corner of Darius's mouth lifted in what might have been a smile. "Dangerous territory."

Devon laughed, the sound warming in his chest. "I'll take my chances."

He stepped past Darius into the lobby's embracing warmth, the temperature shift immediate and enveloping like stepping into a hot bath. The bass vibrated faintly through the floor beneath his boots, a heartbeat pulsing up through leather soles and into his ankles. Ahead, heavy crimson velvet curtains—the deep, saturated red of fresh pomegranate seeds—rippled with the movement of bodies passing through, each parting offering a brief kaleidoscopic glimpse: a shoulder draped in sequins that caught the light, hands gesturing mid-conversation, the flash of a smile beneath the blue-tinted spotlights beyond.

The wall of photographs caught his attention as it always did—a mosaic of silver frames containing faces and moments preserved in time, yellowing at the edges where decades of cigarette smoke had seeped into the paper. Devon studied them with quiet appreciation beneath the now-pristine ceiling, once stained tobacco-brown but scrubbed clean sometime in the late 2000s when the smoking ban hit. He noticed details he'd missed in previous visits: the glint of defiance in a drag performer's kohl-rimmed eye, a lit Virginia Slim dangling between lacquered nails; the tender clasp of hands during what appeared to be a commitment ceremony beside an overflowing crystal ashtray; Echo standing beside a towering queen in a platinum wig, impossibly elegant even in this snapshot against smoke-fogged mirrors, her high cheekbones catching the light, a glass of amber liquid held between long fingers adorned with a single silver ring shaped like a serpent while her companion exhaled a plume of smoke above their heads.

"Look who's back for more," came a lilting voice from the coat check.

Devon turned to find Marisol regarding him with playful scrutiny, their dark eyes dancing in the amber light. Tonight they wore a vintage silk blouse with an intricate pattern that seemed to shift when they moved—different from the tailored men's waistcoat they'd worn last Thursday—their nails painted a deep burgundy that matched their lips, a subtle stubble intentionally visible along their defined jawline.

"That foreman's jacket is still doing things for your shoulders," Marisol continued, leaning forward over the counter. "You know what they say about a man who knows how to work with his hands." Marisol winked, their gaze traveling appreciatively along the breadth of his shoulders beneath the worn leather.

Devon laughed, the sound rolling easily from his chest. He shrugged out of his jacket, comfortable in the familiar ritual of their exchange. "And what exactly do they say, Marisol?"

"That depends entirely on what you're building." They took his jacket with practiced grace, their fingers brushing his deliberately. "Or tearing down."

"Tonight I'm just looking to unwind." He handed over his jacket, feeling the weight lift from his shoulders. The club's warmth seeped into his skin, a welcome contrast to the January chill.

"Aren't we all?" Marisol hung his jacket with theatrical flourish, turning back to slide a brass token across the counter. "Though some of us are better at admitting what we're really searching for."

Devon pocketed the token, feeling its familiar weight. "And what am I searching for, according to your expert analysis?"

"Something real." Marisol's playfulness softened for just a moment, their eyes holding his with unexpected directness. "You're not here for the quick thrills like most of them. I've got eyes, Devon Carter."

The observation landed closer to home than Devon expected. He maintained his easy smile, but something tightened in his chest. "Maybe I just appreciate the music."

"And I'm just a coat check attendant." Marisol's laugh sparkled in the amber light. "Go on in. Echo's been asking after you."

That caught him by surprise. "Echo has?"

"Don't look so shocked. She notices the ones who keep coming back." Marisol gestured toward the velvet curtains with a flick of their wrist. "Especially the ones who watch more than they participate."

Devon nodded, his throat suddenly dry. The brass token felt heavy in his pocket, a small weight anchoring him to reality while Marisol's words seemed to peel back layers he'd thought well-concealed. He moved toward the curtains with deliberate steps, the polished floor reflecting fractured light beneath his boots. The crimson velvet hung before him like a threshold to another world, while behind him, he could feel Marisol's knowing gaze tracking his retreat—gentle but unflinching, like a spotlight he couldn't quite escape.

The Glass Heel opened before him in a rush of sound and sensation as he pushed through the velvet barrier. The bass hit him first—a physical force that vibrated up through the worn leather soles of his steel-toed boots and rattled his ribcage. Then came the complex layering of scents: vanilla-infused perfume, the salt of honest sweat, gin and tonic spilled across sticky tabletops, and something less tangible—possibility hanging in the air like smoke from a forgotten cigarette. Bodies moved on the dance floor beneath cobalt spotlights, their silhouettes creating kaleidoscopic patterns that shifted and reformed with each thunderous beat, arms raised toward the ceiling like worshippers at an altar.

He paused at the threshold, squinting as his pupils contracted against the strobing lights. Devon took in the room with the methodical assessment that had become second nature through years of construction work—identifying support beams, noting exit routes, gauging structural integrity. The crowd filled perhaps two-thirds of the available space—not the sardine-packed weekend crush, but substantial enough that conversations merged into a continuous hum beneath the music. Heather commanded the elevated DJ booth, her box braids with purple ends falling across one eye as her ring-laden fingers moved over turntables and sliders with the precision of a surgeon, her head nodding slightly to a rhythm only she could anticipate, three beats ahead of everyone else.

Devon made his way toward the sweeping counter of poured concrete, its surface embedded with shards of mirror that glittered like stars under the lights, exchanging nods with a cluster of leather-jacketed regulars near the pool table and a silver-haired woman whose septum piercing caught the light when she laughed. Not friends, not exactly, but familiar strangers whose faces he'd come to expect, like the constellation of water rings marking the bartop's varnish. He claimed an empty spot between a couple deep in whispered conversation and a solitary woman nursing something electric blue, resting his forearms against the cool concrete worn smooth by thousands of elbows, and caught Julian's eye through the forest of upturned glasses hanging from the ceiling rack.

"The usual?" Julian asked, already reaching for a glass.

"Yeah, thanks." Devon appreciated the easy familiarity, the lack of need to specify. Six visits had established his preference—a local amber ale, nothing fancy.

Julian set the beer in front of him, amber liquid catching the light. "How's the job site?"

"Coming along." Devon took a grateful sip, the hoppy bitterness washing away the taste of drywall dust that seemed permanently lodged in his throat these days. "Final inspection next week if the weather holds."

He leaned into the comfortable rhythm of the bar, one boot hooked on the brass rail running along the floor, forearms resting on the concrete counter. The day's tension began to unwind from his shoulders. The music shifted—something with a deeper bass line that vibrated up through his planted foot. His attention drifted across the room, taking in the ebb and flow of bodies, the pockets of conversation, the subtle choreography of strangers finding their place in the shared space.

"Devon."

The voice beside him carried warmth and subtle authority, like honey poured over granite. He turned to find Echo standing there, her six-foot frame somehow both imposing and graceful. Tonight she wore a dress that seemed to capture darkness itself—black silk shot through with silver filaments that transformed with every movement. The fabric embraced her frame before cascading into an uneven hem, playing with the club's blue lights like ripples across deep water at midnight, both swallowing and throwing back the glow in impossible ways. Silver cuffs adorned her wrists, a stark contrast to her usual vintage aesthetic. Her raven-black hair hung loose tonight instead of in her signature rolls, framing her face in soft waves. Her silver-gray eyes—unusual against her mahogany skin—held his with the practiced assessment of someone who missed nothing and revealed only what she chose.

"Echo," he nodded, straightening slightly. "Good to see you."

"The feeling is mutual." Her smile was genuine but measured. "Julian taking care of you?"

"Always does." Devon lifted his glass in small salute.

Echo's gaze swept over him with quiet assessment. "Six visits in two months. You're becoming a familiar face around here."

"Trying to," he admitted. Something about Echo invited honesty without demanding it.

"Good." She placed a hand briefly on his shoulder, the touch light but deliberate. "The Heel reveals itself slowly to those who keep returning. Patience is rewarded here."

Before he could respond, she was already turning away, drawn to another corner of her domain where a small commotion had broken out near the DJ booth. The brief interaction left Devon with the distinct impression of having passed some unspoken test—acknowledged but not yet fully accepted, seen but still being evaluated.

He took another sip of his beer, letting the bitter notes of hops bloom across his tongue like an argument that resolves itself. The bar hummed with kinetic energy around him—laughter punctuating the bass line, ice clinking against glass, the percussion of bottles being set down too hard. Three stools down, Miko's tattooed forearms flexed as she shook a silver tumbler with practiced precision, her jade bracelet catching blue light as she poured something electric green over crushed ice for a couple so entangled they seemed to share one shadow.

Devon pushed away from the bar, condensation from his glass cooling his calloused palm. The day's labor—scaling aluminum ladders that left metallic dust on his jeans, hefting fifty-pound drywall sheets until his shoulders burned—had settled into his muscles like a memory. Even now, with sawdust still embedded in the creases of his knuckles, his body hummed with restless electricity. The dance floor beckoned with its pulsing cobalt glow—not to participate, not yet, but to observe from its edges where the bass vibrated through the worn leather soles of his boots and into the marrow of his bones.

He found a spot against a column where the shadows offered a perfect vantage point. From here, he could watch without being watched, could absorb the rhythm without surrendering to it completely. The dancers moved with abandon, bodies writing stories in the blue light—some seeking connection, others losing themselves entirely in the music Heather wove from her booth above.

Devon took a long pull from his beer, the cold

bitterness sliding down his throat as his gaze traveled the perimeter of the floor. There was an honesty here that drew him back week after week. In the careful architecture of his daily life—the measured words with clients, the precise calculations of load-bearing walls—he rarely found spaces where people moved without pretense.

The song shifted, something with a deeper bass line that reverberated in his chest cavity like distant thunder trapped beneath his ribs. Devon closed his eyes for a moment, letting the sensation wash through him, the vibration traveling up from the soles of his steel-toed boots to the base of his skull. When he opened them again, his attention caught on movement near the entrance—a ripple in the blue-tinged darkness.

She stood just beyond the heavy velvet curtain, one hand still touching the fabric as if anchoring herself, hesitating at the threshold between observer and participant. Even in the dim light, Devon recognized her—the woman from his last two visits, with her copper-brown hair that caught the strobing lights and her shoulders that always seemed to carry an invisible weight. Lily. He'd overheard her name during her exchange with Julian last week, the syllables lingering in his memory like the aftertaste of good whiskey.

Tonight she wore a silver-threaded dress that caught the blue light when she moved—a silken waterfall that transformed her willowy frame into something almost ethereal, the fabric clinging then releasing with each step. But it was her face that held his attention: the slight furrow between auburn brows, the way her amber-flecked eyes swept the room with that same careful assessment he recognized in himself. Her gaze paused at each exit, lingered on each unfamiliar face, cataloging threats and escape routes. Looking for danger, yes, but the slight parting of her rose-tinted lips betrayed she was looking for possibility too.

She had barely taken three measured steps inside when Julian appeared, towel slung over his shoulder, moving with the easy confidence of someone who knew exactly where they belonged. He intercepted her with a smile that seemed reserved just for her, leaning in close to speak words Devon couldn't hear. She nodded, the sharp line of her collarbone softening as Julian's hand found the small of her back, guiding her toward the bar. Her silver stiletto heels made barely a sound against the worn hardwood as they crossed the floor together. At the bar, Julian's hands moved in practiced rhythm, amber liquid flowing into a glass with a twist of something citrus, before he offered the drink to her with a slight bow.

There was something about her that resonated with him—the watchfulness, perhaps. The way her fingers drummed a silent rhythm against the glass, how she positioned herself with her back to the wall, one foot slightly turned toward the exit. The sense of someone navigating a space where they weren't yet certain of their welcome. Or maybe it was simpler than that. Maybe it was just the way she held herself apart while clearly longing to belong, evident in how her eyes lingered wistfully on laughing groups before skittering away, a hunger in her gaze that matched the hollow space beneath his own ribs.

Devon set his beer down, suddenly self-conscious of his fixed stare. The Glass Heel wasn't a place for him to project his longings onto strangers, yet he couldn't tear his eyes away as Lily's lips met the rim of Julian's carefully crafted drink. The four of them—Julian, Miko, Echo, and Lily—clustered briefly at the bar, voices and laughter mingling until the moment dissolved, leaving

Lily by herself. Her eyes wandered toward the dancers, bodies moving like living shadows under cobalt light.

It was always like this—the same choreographed dance performed under different neon signs, against different lacquered bars, between different bodies moving like shadows. Devon had lost count of how many sticky-floored clubs, mahogany-topped bars, and velvet-roped lounges he'd drifted through over the years, each one's throbbing bass promising connection but delivering only fleeting touches that evaporated with the morning light, leaving behind nothing but wrinkled sheets and the lingering scent of a stranger's perfume. The Glass Heel carved its own silhouette against that backdrop, though. Here, beneath the cobalt lights that caught in condensation droplets on glass rims, people's eyes held questions that couldn't be answered in a single night.

As he watched Lily at the bar, something unfurled in his chest—recognition, perhaps, like finding a reflection in unexpected water. The careful three-fingered grip she maintained on her tumbler, how her amber-flecked gaze swept the room with that precise mixture of hope and hesitation, lingering on exit signs before returning to the dance floor. She wasn't here for a quick hookup; that much was evident in the way she kept a calculated inch of space between herself and the bar, her silver dress catching light but her shoulders angled slightly away from approaching conversations. The polished exterior—the dress's threads glimmering like captured stars, the deliberate straightness of her spine—stood at odds with the soft vulnerability pooling in her eyes as she surveyed the writhing crowd.

Devon had confronted that same contradiction in his bathroom mirror too many times to count, watching his reflection adjust shirt collars and practice smiles that never quite reached his eyes. The bone-deep exhaustion of constructing a facade brick by careful brick, mortared with casual laughter and maintained with practiced charm, while something altogether different stirred beneath that surface. The familiar heaviness of conversations that skated across weather and careers but never ventured into the territories mapped by the lines etched beside his eyes.

And then, as if pulled by some invisible thread, her eyes found his across the room.

The connection was immediate and electric, traveling the distance between them like a current. For one suspended moment, they simply looked at each other, acknowledgment passing between them without words.

Something in her eyes told him that she wanted to look away, but she couldn't—a flutter of panic in those amber-flecked irises, like a bird suddenly aware of its cage, wings beating against invisible bars. Her pupils dilated slightly in the low light, creating dark pools ringed by honey-gold, and in that expanding darkness he recognized a mirror of his own reluctant fascination. The slight tremor in her lashes as she blinked once, twice, betrayed the internal struggle between caution and curiosity, between the safety of anonymity and the dangerous thrill of being truly seen.

He peeled himself away from the column where the cool concrete had been seeping through his shirt, drawn forward by a curiosity that overrode his usual caution like high tide washing over sea walls. The crowd between them pulsed and swayed, a living kaleidoscope of limbs and torsos moving to Heather's thunderous bass drops that vibrated the very floorboards beneath his feet. Through gaps in the writhing bodies, he kept his eyes fixed on Lily, watching how the blue lights caught in her copper hair when she turned her head. She was feigning interest in the dancers now, her fingertip tracing the condensation on her glass, but every thirty seconds or so, her gaze would flick in his direction—quick, furtive glances that lasted just long enough to confirm he was still coming before darting away like startled fish.

Devon traced the edge of the dance floor, a satellite in steady orbit. Bodies pressed against him—a shoulder here, an elbow there—as he maintained his deliberate pace along the perimeter. Each footfall synchronized with the club's heartbeat, bass notes vibrating through his leather soles. He kept his trajectory clear but unhurried, eyes never wavering from her despite the strobing cobalt lights. This wasn't pursuit but invitation, his measured approach offering her the dignity of choice: meet him halfway or slip away unscathed.

She didn't move. Instead, he caught her stealing glances at him between sips of her drink, the amber liquid catching blue reflections as she tilted the crystal tumbler to her lips. Her copper hair fell in a curtain across one shoulder when she turned her head, tracking his progress while maintaining the pretense of casual observation. One silver stiletto tapped almost imperceptibly against the bar rail. The game was familiar but somehow fresher here, weighted with possibility rather than inevitable conclusion.

Devon closed the distance between them with each deliberate step, his mind racing ahead of his feet. What would he say to her? Something casual but confident. Not a line—he'd never been that guy—but something honest that might open a real conversation. Yet hadn't every "real" conversation he'd initiated in places like this eventually dissolved into disappointment? The usual club opener felt too shallow for a woman who seemed to be seeking the same elusive connection he was, but maybe that shallowness was protective—for both of them.

He watched as she lifted her glass to her lips, the amber liquid catching cobalt light like a trapped sunset. Her eyes—those honey-gold irises ringed with chestnut—darted toward him, then away again, her spine straightening with the precision of a dancer finding her mark. The silver fabric of her dress rippled with the movement, momentarily transforming her into a mercury sculpture against the concrete bar. She knew he was coming. The awareness between them stretched taut as piano wire, vibrating with unplayed notes that seemed to hum beneath the club's thunderous bass.

Three more steps. Two.

Devon felt a strange calm settle over him as he reached the edge of her space—a pocket of stillness amid the club's chaos, like stepping into the eye of a hurricane. The frantic calculations that usually raced through his mind before approaching someone new had quieted to a whisper beneath the steady rhythm of his heartbeat. No rehearsed lines balanced on his tongue, no strategic angles to consider. Just the simple truth of two people who had noticed each other across a crowded room, their gazes cutting through the blue-tinted darkness like searchlights finding harbor.

Lily looked up at his approach, her fingers tightening around her glass until her knuckles bloomed white against the crystal. The pulse at her throat fluttered visibly beneath skin that caught the cobalt light like polished alabaster, betraying the composure she tried to maintain with her carefully squared shoulders and lifted chin. Her eyes—not hazel as he'd thought from across the room, but a complex amber with fragments of green near the pupils—met his directly now, no more stolen glances. They held both challenge and question in their depths, like someone standing at the edge of a high dive, simultaneously afraid of the fall and already committed to the leap.

"I'm Devon," he said, his voice pitched just loud enough to carry over the music without shouting. He didn't offer his hand, didn't lean into her space, just stood solid and present. "I've seen you here before. Thought it was time I introduced myself."

The directness seemed to catch her off guard. She blinked, a smile tugging at the corner of her mouth—surprise mixed with something that might have been relief.

"Lily," she replied, her voice steadier than he expected. "I've noticed you too."

Her words hung suspended in the blue-tinted air between them, an unexpected honesty that sliced through the usual club pretense like sunlight through morning fog. Devon felt something loosen in his chest—the first knot of tension unwinding, a physical sensation like a fist slowly unclenching beneath his sternum. The tightness that had been coiling between his shoulder blades since he'd spotted her across the room melted away, leaving behind a curious lightness that spread through his ribcage with each breath.

Chapter 3

Sparks at the Glass Heel

Lily sipped her whiskey, savoring the burn that bloomed into caramel sweetness as she stole a glance at Devon. He'd claimed the weathered leather stool next to hers, one sleeve pushed up to reveal ink faded by years of sunlight. Between them lay six precise inches of emptiness—a gap small enough to cross in a heartbeat, yet vast as an ocean with all they weren't saying. The air seemed to crackle there, charged with potential like the weighted silence before thunder.

"So," Devon said, his voice a low rumble that she felt more than heard over the music, "third visit?"

Lily's eyebrows rose. "You've been keeping track?"

"Not exactly." His lips curved into a smile that made something flutter in her chest. "Just noticed you. The way you watch everything from the edges before diving in."

Heat crept up Lily's neck in a slow, treacherous wave that had nothing to do with the bourbon. Her skin prickled beneath her collar as if traced by an invisible finger, and she fought the urge to press her cool glass against her burning cheek. The idea that he'd been watching her while she'd been watching him created a strange, circular intimacy—like accidentally catching your own reflection in a mirror you didn't know was there, only to find someone else's eyes meeting yours in the glass.

"Takes one to know one," she replied, surprising herself with her boldness. "You're not exactly the center-of-attention type yourself."

Devon's laugh was genuine, his shoulders relaxing slightly. "Guilty as charged."

Julian materialized behind the bar, his tattooed forearms flexing as he slid a fresh amber beer toward Devon without being asked. The glass left a glistening trail across the bar. His dark eyes, lined with the faintest crow's feet that crinkled when he smiled, moved between them with undisguised interest, like a chess player who'd just witnessed a particularly intriguing opening move.

"I see you two finally found each other," he said, leaning his elbows on the polished concrete bar. "Took you long enough."

Lily nearly choked on her drink. "What's that supposed to mean?"

"It means," Julian said, his voice dropping conspiratorially, "that I've watched you both circling this place like sharks for weeks, noticing everything but never quite diving in." His gaze shifted to Devon. "And both stealing glances when you think the other isn't looking."

Devon ran a hand over his stubbled chin, a gesture Lily immediately read as self-conscious. "Your imagination's working overtime, Julian."

"Is it though?" Julian's smile was knowing as he began wiping down the bar with practiced efficiency. "The Glass Heel has a way of bringing together people who are looking for the same thing."

"And what exactly are we looking for?" Lily challenged, though her heart hammered against her ribs.

Julian's eyes softened. "Something real. Something that lasts longer than a night." He straightened, tossing the towel over his shoulder. "Or maybe just someone who sees past all the..." he gestured vaguely at Lily's dress, at Devon's carefully maintained exterior, "...the armor."

Lily glanced at Devon, finding his eyes already on her—warm amber in this light, steady and unblinking. A current passed between them, electric and undeniable, raising goosebumps along her forearms. His pupils dilated slightly, and the corner of his mouth twitched with the ghost of a smile that acknowledged what they both felt: the unsettling intimacy of being read like a book whose pages you thought were closed to strangers.

"Well," Devon said after Julian moved away to serve another customer, "that was subtle."

Lily laughed, the tension breaking. "About as subtle as a wrecking ball."

"Julian means well," Devon said, taking a sip of his beer. "He's got this thing about connections. Thinks it's his personal mission to foster them."

"Is that what this is? A connection?" The words slipped out before Lily could stop them.

Devon held her gaze, his expression thoughtful as he considered her question. "I think it could be," he said finally. "If we wanted it to be."

His directness struck her like a physical force—no pretense, no careful dance of half-truths, just raw honesty laid bare between them. It made Lily's chest tighten with an unfamiliar ache, as if some long-dormant muscle was being stretched for the first time. She took another sip of her bourbon, letting the amber liquid coat her tongue and burn a path down her throat, hoping the familiar sensation would anchor her against this unexpected tide of vulnerability.

"So what do you do when you're not analyzing people at The Glass Heel?" Devon asked, shifting the conversation to safer ground.

"I'm a corporate paralegal at Matthews & Doyle," Lily said, tucking a strand of hair behind her ear. "Mid-sized firm downtown. Lots of contract review, due diligence, the occasional rush filing that keeps me at my desk until midnight."

"Sounds demanding."

"It can be. But it's stable." She traced the rim of her glass with her fingertip. "What about you?"

"Construction management," Devon replied. "Currently overseeing a renovation of a historic theater in Wicker Park. Lots of unexpected challenges when you're dealing with a building from the 1920s."

"That sounds fascinating actually," Lily said, genuinely interested. "Do you like it?"

"I love the problem-solving aspect. Each day brings

something new." His eyes lit up as he spoke, and Lily found herself drawn to that spark of passion. "There's something deeply satisfying about preserving these old spaces while giving them new life."

Lily nodded, understanding exactly what he meant. "Creating something that lasts."

"Exactly." Devon looked at her with renewed interest, as if surprised by how quickly she'd grasped what drove him.

As they talked, Lily felt something shift between them—the initial awkwardness melting away like ice in warm whiskey, giving way to a conversational rhythm that felt surprisingly natural. Devon asked thoughtful questions that peeled back her carefully constructed layers, his amber eyes holding hers with an intensity that made her skin prickle. When she spoke, he leaned forward slightly, the leather of his stool creaking beneath him, his fingers absently tracing the condensation rings on the bar. Not once did his attention wander to scan the room or check his phone, which lay face-down beside his half-empty glass. It was disarming, being the focus of such undivided interest, like standing in a spotlight she hadn't auditioned for.

Suddenly, Devon noticed Lily's eyes flick over his shoulder, her expression changing subtly. She straightened almost imperceptibly, her spine stiffening beneath her silk blouse, a hint of color touching her cheeks like watercolor bleeding across paper.

Devon turned, following her gaze to find Echo watching them from across the room. The club owner stood near the DJ booth, resplendent in her dress that seemed to absorb and reflect light in impossible ways. When their eyes met, Echo's crimson lips curved into a small, knowing smile—the kind that suggested she was pleased with a plan coming together exactly as she'd envisioned.

Devon turned back to Lily, who looked both embarrassed at being caught staring and slightly awed.

"She has that effect on everyone," he said with a soft laugh. "Echo's presence is... magnetic."

"It's not just that," Lily admitted. "It's like she sees right through you, but in a way that makes you feel recognized rather than exposed."

Devon nodded, understanding exactly what she meant. "I admire her tremendously. What she's built here, the sanctuary she's created—it's remarkable," Devon continued, then turned back to Lily, his voice softening. "But I have to admit, impressive as Echo is, she's not the one who's had my attention these past few weeks."

The directness of his gaze made Lily's breath catch in her throat like a bird suddenly caged. The bourbon's warmth—that familiar amber glow that usually spread from her chest to her fingertips—couldn't compete with the heat rising to her face, a flush that crept up her neck and bloomed across her cheeks like watercolor on wet paper.

"I've been coming back hoping to see you," he added, his voice low enough that only she could hear it. "Watching you watch the room. Wondering what you were looking for."

Lily's fingers tightened around her glass, the condensation cool against her skin as her knuckles whitened. Her pulse quickened beneath the delicate skin of her wrist. This kind of honesty was unfamiliar territory—like stepping onto a frozen lake where the ice might hold or might crack beneath her weight. No carefully constructed defenses, no choreographed dance of half-truths, just a simple truth laid bare between them, fragile and dangerous as a lit match.

"Would you like to dance?" Devon asked, nodding toward the floor where bodies moved in fluid synchronicity to Heather's latest track.

The question hung between them, weighted with possibility like a crystal pendant catching light. Lily hesitated, her fingers tightening around the smooth curve of her glass. The bar had been her fortress all evening—between her and the world, Julian's watchful presence a comforting sentinel. Out there on the dance floor, bodies moved in liquid synchronicity under blue-violet lights, a sea she'd have to navigate without armor. Her silk dress suddenly felt too thin, her carefully applied lipstick too bright.

"I'm not very good," she admitted.

Devon's smile was gentle. "Neither am I. We can be not very good together."

He stood and extended his hand, palm up—an invitation rather than an insistence. The amber light from the bar caught the fine lines etched across his skin. Lily took a final sip of her bourbon for courage, the last drop burning a golden path down her throat, then placed her hand in his. His palm was warm and slightly calloused against her manicured fingers, the grip firm but gentle as he led her through the maze of bodies toward the pulsing heart of the club.

The bass vibrated through the soles of Lily's three-inch heels as they found a spot at the edge of the crowd where indigo lights swirled like underwater currents. Devon turned to face her, the blue light playing across the sharp angles of his face, softening the cleft in his chin and deepening the shadows beneath his cheekbones. For a moment, they stood awkwardly, the six inches between them feeling both vast and microscopic, the reality of their bodies in this shared space suddenly more intimate than their conversation had been.

Devon moved first, his broad shoulders finding the rhythm while his feet stayed planted on the sticky floor. Lily mirrored him, keeping a careful distance between them, her silk dress whispering against her thighs. Her movements felt stiff, mechanical, like a wind-up doll with rusted joints. She couldn't remember the last time she'd danced with anyone, let alone a near-stranger who looked at her with such undisguised interest, his amber eyes never leaving her face even as the crowd surged around them like a restless tide.

"Relax," Devon said, leaning closer to be heard over the music. "Nobody's watching us."

"You don't know that," Lily countered, but she felt a smile tugging at her lips.

"I do, actually." His eyes crinkled at the corners. "They're all too busy trying not to be watched themselves."

The observation broke something loose in Lily's chest—a knot of tension she hadn't realized was there until it unraveled. She laughed, the sound bubbling up unexpectedly like champagne breaching the surface, and let her hips sway more freely to the beat. The silk of her dress slid against her thighs with each movement. Devon's smile widened in response, teeth flashing white against his dark skin, the amber flecks in his eyes catching the indigo lights as his own movements became more fluid, shoulders rolling with newfound confidence.

The song shifted—something slower, with a deeper bass line that vibrated through the soles of her feet and up her calves, the rhythm like a physical force drawing them toward each other. Devon's hand found the small of her back, his palm warm through the thin fabric, fingers splayed in a question made of gentle pressure. Lily stepped forward in answer, closing the distance between them until she could feel the heat radiating from his body, smell the faint notes of cedar and citrus on his skin.

"Better?" he asked, his breath warm against her ear.

"Much," Lily murmured, surprising herself with how easily the admission came.

As the music flowed around them like warm honey, something shifted in their movements. Devon's hand at her waist became less tentative, his fingers spreading slightly to draw her closer, the heat of his palm burning through the delicate silk of her dress. Lily found herself responding, her body softening against his as the careful distance between them dissolved into nothing but shared breath and synchronized heartbeats.

She caught his eye and held it this time, not glancing away as she had earlier. The electric blue light caught the sharp angles of his face, shadowing the hollow beneath his cheekbones and illuminating the faint stubble along his jaw in turns as they moved together. His eyes—amber flecked with gold—crinkled at the corners when he smiled down at her, and Lily felt an answering smile spread across her own face, her lipstick slightly faded from her earlier drinks.

"You lied," she said, leaning up to speak near his ear, her lips almost brushing his skin. "You're actually quite good at this."

Devon's laugh rumbled through his chest, vibrating against her palm where it rested. "The right partner makes all the difference."

His hand traced a slow path up her spine, leaving warmth in its wake. Lily caught glimpses of their reflection in the mirrored column nearby—his dark fingers splayed against the pale silk of her dress, the contrast striking and beautiful. When his fingers reached the nape of her neck, they lingered there against her fair skin, a gentle pressure that sent shivers cascading down her arms.

The song shifted again, the DJ transitioning into a pulsing house track with staccato beats that ricocheted off the club's mirrored walls. Despite the tempo change, neither of them broke apart. Instead, Devon spun her unexpectedly—his movement precise and controlled, his palm guiding the small of her back with just enough pressure to set her in motion without forcing it. The silk of Lily's dress flared around her thighs as she twirled, catching sapphire light in its folds. She laughed, the sound bubbling up from somewhere long dormant inside her, as she came back to him in a fluid arc, her hand finding the solid curve of his shoulder, fingers pressing into the warm cotton of his shirt, steadying herself against the pleasant dizziness.

"Where did that come from?" she asked, breathless.

"Hidden talents," he replied with a wink that made her stomach flip. "I'm full of surprises."

They fell into a playful rhythm, her silk dress whispering against her calves as they moved. His fingers splayed across the small of her back, the heat of his palm penetrating the thin fabric while his thumb traced deliberate circles that sent shivers up her spine. Each subtle pressure guided her through the crowd of writhing bodies, the bass thrumming beneath their feet like a second heartbeat.

Lily found herself mesmerized by the soft curve of

his lower lip, the way one corner lifted slightly higher than the other when he smiled, revealing a dimple that carved a perfect crescent into his right cheek. Under the shifting indigo lights, his amber eyes caught flecks of gold that seemed to dance with the music. She no longer ducked away from his gaze—instead, she drank it in, tilting her chin down to meet it. When their eyes locked, she held the connection until the air between them felt electric, charged with unspoken possibilities.

After executing a complex turn that left her momentarily breathless, Devon pulled her toward him. She collided softly against his chest, her chin dipping to rest against the crown of his head. His arms encircled her waist while hers draped naturally across his shoulders, her three-inch heels accentuating the height difference between them. As they stood motionless amid the sea of dancers, she felt the solid warmth of him against her collarbone, his heartbeat vibrating through her sternum—strong and slightly erratic, perfectly synchronized with the wild flutter of her own.

"This is nice," he said, his voice low beside her ear. The simple honesty of it made her chest tighten.

"Yes," she agreed, allowing her cheek to rest against his shoulder for a moment. "It is."

His hand found hers, fingers intertwining with a sureness that belied their short acquaintance—his palm calloused but warm, his grip neither too tight nor too tentative. Lily looked down at their joined hands, struck by how the deep umber of his skin contrasted with her pale fingers, how his thumb traced an unconscious half-circle against her wrist where her pulse fluttered like a trapped bird.

As the song built toward its crescendo, the crowd pressed closer, bodies moving with increasing abandon.

Perfumes mingled with sweat in a heady cloud while strobe lights carved the dancers into stop-motion silhouettes. The heat and proximity became suddenly overwhelming, the air thick as syrup in her lungs. Lily felt sweat beading at her temples, dampening the fine hairs at the nape of her neck, her breath coming faster as the space between strangers disappeared into a single undulating mass.

"Need some air?" Devon asked, noticing her discomfort before she could voice it.

Lily nodded gratefully. "Please."

Devon kept hold of her hand as he guided her through the press of dancers, creating a path with his solid presence. They emerged from the dance floor into a quieter corner near one of the sapphire-upholstered booths. A small table stood empty, as if waiting just for them. Devon gestured toward it with a questioning look, and Lily sank gratefully onto the cushioned seat.

"Better?" he asked, sliding in beside her.

"Much." She pressed her palms against the cool surface of the table, centering herself. "I forget sometimes how intense it gets in there."

Devon nodded, studying her face. "You looked a million miles away for a second."

The observation was gentle but perceptive. Lily hesitated, weighing how much to share. Something about Devon's steady presence made her want to be honest in a way she rarely allowed herself.

"I was thinking about work, actually," she admitted. "How different this feels."

"Different how?"

Lily traced a pattern on the table's surface with her

fingertip. "At the firm, I'm practically invisible. I do good work—great work, actually—but it's like I'm a ghost moving through the office." The words came easier than she expected, tumbling out like they'd been waiting for permission. "I spend my days surrounded by people who look through me, not at me. Partners who can't remember my name even though I've saved their asses on deadlines for three years."

Devon's eyes never left her face as she spoke, his attention unwavering.

"Here, with you..." She gestured between them. "It's the first time in months I've felt like someone is actually seeing me."

The admission hung in the air between them, more vulnerable than she'd intended. Lily felt heat creep up her neck, regretting her candor.

"I know exactly what you mean," Devon said, his voice quiet but firm. "Being seen for who you actually are, not just what people expect."

He leaned back slightly, his shoulders straightening. "People take one look at me and make assumptions. I'm five-six in boots on a good day." A wry smile touched his lips. "In construction, that means I'm constantly proving myself. Guys see me walk onto a site and immediately think I can't handle the physical demands."

His hand rested on the table between them, strong fingers curled loosely. "They don't realize I can deadlift more than most men a foot taller. That I've spent my life developing strength that doesn't show in height."

Lily studied him with new appreciation, noticing how his frame, though compact, radiated a solid strength. The fabric of his shirt stretched taut across his chest when he leaned forward, revealing the outline of muscles honed by years of physical labor rather than vanity workouts. His forearms, exposed by rolled sleeves, were corded with veins that ran like rivers beneath skin burnished by outdoor work. She could see it now in the set of his shoulders—squared and steady as foundation stones—and in the quiet confidence of his movements, each gesture precise and economical, wasting neither energy nor space.

"I get that," she said softly. "Being reduced to what people see, not who you are."

Around them, the crowd had begun to thin slightly, like foam receding from shoreline after high tide. Couples drifted toward the exits in twos and threes, leaving expanding islands of empty space on the dance floor. The music shifted to something with a slower, more hypnotic beat—all liquid bass and whispered vocals that seemed to curl around the remaining dancers like smoke. Lily glanced at her slim gold watch, its face catching the indigo light as she tilted her wrist. The delicate hands pointed well past midnight, the realization landing with a soft shock that made her blink twice.

"People are leaving," she observed, watching as couples and groups drifted toward the exit.

Devon nodded. "Thursday night. Work tomorrow for most people." He studied her face. "Do you need to go?"

The question hung between them, weighted with possibility. Lily considered her early meeting, the stack of contracts waiting on her desk. Then she looked at Devon—really looked at him—and shook her head.

"Not yet," she said, and was rewarded with a smile that made her glad she'd stayed.

They fell into conversation again, easier now after

their shared confidences on the dance floor. Devon told her about the theater renovation, his eyes lighting up as he described uncovering original plasterwork hidden beneath decades of cheap renovations. Lily found herself laughing at his impression of the building's owner, a eccentric millionaire with very specific ideas about historical preservation.

"He wanted to keep the original wiring," Devon said, shaking his head in disbelief. "Actual knob and tube from 1924. I had to explain that if he did that, his beautiful theater would probably burn to the ground within a year."

"Did he listen?"

"Eventually. After I brought in three separate electrical inspectors to tell him the same thing." Devon's laugh was warm, inviting her to share in the absurdity. "People get attached to the strangest things."

Lily took a sip of water from the glass Julian had silently delivered during their conversation. "What about you? What are you attached to?"

Devon considered the question, his expression thoughtful. "Authenticity, I think. In buildings and in people." His eyes met hers. "I like things that are exactly what they appear to be."

The words settled between them like stones dropping into still water, and Lily felt her chest tighten, her lungs constricting beneath the silky fabric of her silver dress. She wondered if he could see the parts of herself she kept carefully hidden—the dog-eared résumés stashed in her desk drawer, the browser tabs of apartments in other cities, the uncertainties that left her staring at her ceiling until three a.m. most nights.

Before she could respond, the music shifted

again—something slower, with a sultry bass line that crawled up through the soles of her heels and vibrated in her ankles, her calves, her thighs. The lights dimmed further, casting everyone in amber and indigo shadows. Devon's eyes, dark as wet cedar, flickered toward the dance floor where couples were drawing closer together, then back to her, his pupils dilated in the low light.

"Would you like to dance again?" he asked, his voice lower than before.

Lily hesitated only briefly before nodding. "I'd like that."

As they rose, Lily caught sight of Echo across the room. The club owner stood near the DJ booth, her silver-gray eyes gleaming like polished river stones beneath the pulsing indigo lights. Her obsidian hair was swept up in an elaborate twist that accentuated her high cheekbones and the long, elegant column of her neck. When she noticed Lily watching, Echo inclined her head slightly—the barest tilt of her chin, yet somehow regal, deliberate, like a queen bestowing favor.

Devon's hand found hers, his calloused palm sliding against her softer skin, fingers interlacing with a perfect pressure—neither too possessive nor too tentative. The dance floor opened before them, the crowd having thinned to scattered islands of swaying bodies. The air between dancers hung heavy with perfume, aftershave, and the sweet musk of exertion. Lily felt Echo's gaze following them, a tangible weight between her shoulder blades, propelling her forward.

This time, when Devon's arms circled her waist, she moved into his embrace without hesitation. His hands settled at the small of her back where her silver dress dipped low, his fingertips warm against her bare skin. The music pulsed around them, a slow, hypnotic beat that vibrated through the soles of her stilettos and up into her bones. Lily's hands slid up to rest on his shoulders, feeling the solid strength beneath her fingertips, the subtle shift of muscle beneath crisp cotton.

"You're not as invisible as you think," Devon murmured, his breath warm against her ear.

Lily's heart stuttered in her chest. "No?"

"I saw you the first night you came here." His hand traced a slow path up her spine, each touch deliberate. "Standing by the bar, taking everything in. You were the most interesting person in the room."

Heat bloomed across her skin. The admission should have made her uncomfortable—the idea of being watched, studied—but instead, she felt a strange thrill. In Devon's eyes, she wasn't just seen; she was worth seeing.

Their bodies moved in perfect synchronicity now, the earlier awkwardness completely dissolved. Lily let her cheek rest against his shoulder, breathing in the subtle scent of his cologne mixed with something uniquely him. His hand at her waist drew her closer until the space between them disappeared entirely.

"This feels..." she began, then stopped, unsure how to finish the thought without revealing too much.

"Right?" Devon suggested, his voice a low rumble she felt against her chest.

Lily nodded, not trusting her voice. It did feel right—surprisingly, unexpectedly right—to be in his arms, moving together as if they'd been dancing for years instead of minutes.

The song shifted, blending seamlessly into something even slower, more intimate. Around them, the remaining couples drew closer together, the dance floor becoming a collection of embraces more than movements. Devon's thumb traced small circles at the small of her back, each touch sending tiny sparks along her nerves.

Lily lowered her head to look at him, finding his eyes already on her face. The intensity of his gaze made her breath catch. His hand moved from her back to her face, fingers brushing a strand of hair behind her ear with unexpected tenderness.

"Lily," he said, her name sounding different in his voice—special, significant.

The moment stretched between them, electric with possibility. Lily felt herself leaning closer, drawn by the gravity of his gaze, the warmth of his hand now cradling her cheek.

Then the music stopped abruptly, like a record needle yanked across vinyl. The overhead lights blared to life—clinical fluorescents that transformed the room from velvet shadows to an overexposed photograph. Lily blinked three times in rapid succession, her mascara-heavy lashes fluttering against the assault of brightness. The dance floor, moments ago a secret garden of whispers and touches, now revealed itself as merely scuffed hardwood with spilled drinks glistening in corners. But Devon remained close, his cologne—sandalwood with hints of bergamot—still enveloping her. His hand stayed warm against the silk covering her waist, his thumb pressing just firmly enough to anchor her in the moment while everyone else around them broke apart.

Chapter 4

Frost and Breath

"I'm not ready for this to end," Devon said, his voice low enough that only she could hear.

Lily's pulse quickened. "Neither am I."

Devon's eyes held hers, searching. "Have you heard of the Heel's Nest?"

"The hotel upstairs?" Lily nodded. She'd overheard whispers about it during her previous visits—exclusive rooms above the club, accessible only to certain patrons. "I've never been."

"Me neither." His thumb traced a small circle at her waist. "But tonight feels... special. Maybe we could see if there's a room available."

Heat bloomed across Lily's skin. The suggestion hung between them, weighted with implication but free of pressure. Devon waited, patient, his expression open.

"Yes," she said finally. "I'd like that."

His smile was immediate and warm, crinkling the corners of his eyes where fine lines appeared like delicate tributaries. He took her hand, his fingers—slightly calloused at the tips—intertwining with hers, creating a perfect lattice of skin against skin. They navigated through the thinning crowd, past a woman in a crimson dress who swayed slightly to music only she could still hear, toward the gleaming bar.

Julian was wiping down the polished surface with methodical circular motions, his movements efficient and practiced as he prepared for closing. Under the harsh fluorescents, every water spot and fingerprint on the bar stood out in stark relief, transforming what had been a gleaming altar of possibility into just another surface that needed cleaning. He looked up as they approached, the overhead lights casting unflattering shadows beneath his eyes, a knowing smile playing at his lips, one eyebrow arching slightly upward.

"Let me guess," he said before either could speak. "Not ready to call it a night?"

Devon laughed, squeezing Lily's hand. "That obvious, huh?"

"I've been doing this a long time." Julian set down his towel, leaning forward on his elbows. "You're wondering about the Nest."

Lily felt heat rise to her cheeks but didn't look away. "Is there... availability tonight?"

Julian's expression softened. "The Nest is by invitation only. For patrons Echo knows well." He glanced between them. "You'd need to speak with her directly."

"Is she still here?" Devon asked, his thumb brushing against Lily's knuckles in a gesture that felt both reassuring and electric.

"By the spiral staircase." Julian nodded toward the far corner of the club. "She's always there at closing, watching over her domain."

They thanked him and moved away from the bar, still hand in hand, Devon's thumb occasionally brushing against the delicate bones of her wrist. Lily felt a flutter of nerves in her stomach, like champagne bubbles rising too quickly. What were they doing? She barely knew Devon—just fragments of him: the sandalwood scent of his cologne, the precise way he folded his pocket square, the slight rasp in his laugh after his third beer—and yet here she was, pursuing something that felt both reckless and inevitable, like stepping off a cliff into warm, waiting water.

Echo stood at the foot of an ornate spiral staircase that Lily hadn't noticed before—wrought iron painted midnight blue with gold flecks that caught the light like trapped stars, each step narrowing as it disappeared upward into velvet shadows beyond the club's main floor. She wore her authority like a second skin, her posture both relaxed and vigilant, silver-gray eyes taking in the last moments of the night with the quiet satisfaction of a curator watching patrons appreciate her carefully assembled exhibition.

She turned as they approached, the movement fluid as mercury. Echo's gaze swept over them, her silver-gray eyes—the color of storm clouds backlit by moonlight—lingering on their interlaced fingers. Her crimson lips, the exact shade of the inside of a blood orange, curved into a smile that held both warmth and restraint, as if she were privy to a secret they had yet to discover.

"Devon. Lily." She inclined her head slightly. "I see you found each other at last."

Lily felt Devon's hand tighten around hers. The casual observation from Echo suggested they'd been watched, perhaps even expected to connect. She wasn't sure how that made her feel.

"We were wondering," Devon began, his voice steady despite the slight tension Lily felt in his grip, "about the Nest. If there might be a room available tonight."

Echo's expression softened, but Lily detected a hint of regret before she even spoke. "The Nest is a special sanctuary," Echo said, her voice melodic but firm. "It's reserved for patrons who have demonstrated their commitment to what we've built here." She gestured upward toward the spiral staircase. "Those rooms aren't simply accommodations—they're extensions of the trust we cultivate in these walls."

Lily's heart sank. She understood the unspoken message: they weren't ready yet. Weren't trusted enough.

"How many visits does it take?" Devon asked, his tone respectful despite the disappointment Lily could hear underneath.

Echo laughed softly. "It's not about counting, Devon. It's about belonging." She reached out, her fingers brushing Lily's bare shoulder in a touch that felt both comforting and electric. "When you're ready for the Nest, you'll know. And so will I."

The rejection was gentle but definitive. Lily swallowed her disappointment, nodding her understanding. She had to admit there was something reassuring about Echo's caution—the care taken to preserve what made this place special.

"Thank you for asking," Echo added, her voice warming. "It speaks to what's growing between you." Her gaze moved between them, assessing. "Some connections are worth nurturing slowly."

Devon nodded, his thumb tracing small circles against Lily's palm. "We understand."

"There are other ways to extend an evening," Echo said, her silver-gray eyes softening with understanding. "The Starlight Diner, just two blocks east—they serve the best coffee in the city at any hour." Her crimson lips curved into a genuine smile. "And I promise, they've never turned anyone away for being a first-time customer."

Lily couldn't help but laugh at that, the tension breaking. "Thank you, Echo."

Echo inclined her head again, a silent dismissal that somehow felt like a blessing. As they turned away from the wrought-iron staircase, Lily felt a curious mixture of disappointment and anticipation swirling in her chest, like honey and lemon stirred into hot water.

They retrieved their coats from Marisol at the polished mahogany check stand, who winked at them with undisguised approval, their kohl-rimmed eyes crinkling at the corners. "Next time," they whispered to Lily as she slipped on her cashmere wrap, their warm breath carrying the faint scent of cinnamon. "The Nest is worth waiting for."

The midnight air stung Lily's cheeks as she stepped into it, a sudden, crystalline slap that made her gasp. The shock of cold after the velvet warmth of the club was always more than she'd remembered, as if each exit from The Glass Heel was the first. She fumbled the silk wrap tighter around her, knowing it would do nothing—the chill saw through every barrier, found its way between the threads. But it was ritual, and ritual was something: her hands practiced, tucking the ends, arms crossed high on her chest not just for warmth but to keep herself contained. She felt the urge to shiver, tamped it down, and tried to focus on the faint thrill that still vibrated in her limbs from the music.

The heavy door swung closed with a muted thud, sealing off the club's warmth and leaving them in the night's relative quiet. Through the brick walls came the faint thrum of bass, while somewhere blocks away, a city bus growled to life. Devon tilted his face skyward, letting the cold air wash over him like a verdict. Darius called out a goodnight. Lily studied Devon's expression, searching for traces of frustration or wounded pride after their rejection, but found only calm acceptance as he thanked the man—treating what could have been humiliation as merely a change in plans.

Now he stuffed his hands in his coat pockets, looked at her with an easy smile despite the way his teeth chattered against the cold. "Sorry about the Nest," he said, and his voice came out quieter than usual, a soft rumble that seemed to warm the air between them. "I shouldn't have gotten ahead of myself." No blame, no expectation; he stood in the cold with her, equal partners in misadventure.

She wanted, desperately, to be angry at someone, to press her disappointment into his palm, to transfer the burn from her chest to something outside her. But when she looked at him, she saw only a patient steadiness, a willingness to let the night reshape itself rather than fight it. Maybe that's why she'd come out tonight at all—because Devon had always been a steady hand on the tiller, the one person she could count on not to flinch when things twisted out of control. Even so, her disappointment had a physicality to it, a weight she carried with each step as they started down the steps and onto the sidewalk.

The block in front of The Glass Heel was a makeshift theater of departure: couples in various states of undress shouting for cabs, a trio of twinks in matching leather heading east toward the blue line, a pair of club regulars squeezing each other for warmth as they waited for a rideshare. There was a curl of cigarette smoke from the alley, a hiss of steam from a vent, the distant echo of a car alarm wailing two streets over. Lily watched a woman in a red mini-dress climb into the backseat of a waiting Prius, her laughter bouncing off the frosted brick, and ached to join her—someone who had gotten what she came for.

She had not. The promise of the Nest had hovered all night, a private room above the club, a place to let the evening unspool in safety and candlelight. She had let herself picture it: Devon's hand on the small of her back, the slow unwind of conversation, maybe a kiss that lingered. Instead, she'd been told—politely, always politely—that, no, they couldn't go up tonight. No explanation. Just the gate closing in her face.

"Maybe it's not us," she said, picking at the silk near her wrist. "Maybe it's just that kind of night." She tried to make her tone light, but it landed with a brittle snap.

Devon's smile widened, a flash of teeth that went crooked at the edges. "I've had worse," he said. "Once got locked out of my own apartment at three in the morning in nothing but a towel. My neighbor called the cops. I was on the news for, like, a week."

She snorted, surprised. "You're kidding."

He shook his head, solemn. "Check the archives.

2017, right after Thanksgiving. I made the police blotter."

She laughed then, a real one, and the sound startled her. Maybe the cold was abrading her defenses, or maybe she just needed the pressure release, but as they moved down the block she felt something in her begin to loosen. There was still an ache, yes, but it was a dull one, not the sharp spike it had been.

The sidewalk was sleet-slick, patched with dirty snow that had been trampled down and refrozen into miniature glaciers. Lily's heels were instantly at war with the terrain; she took careful, mincing steps, eyes down, scanning for black ice. Devon offered his arm, a gallant gesture that might have annoyed her in another context, but tonight she took it, wrapping her fingers around the wool of his work coat.

"Those are an accident waiting to happen," he said, nodding toward her feet.

Lily laughed, the tension between them dissolving. "Says the man wearing what appears to be a work coat to a nightclub."

"Hey, this is genuine leather. Vintage." He ran a hand down the worn sleeve with mock defensiveness. "And it's warm, which is more than I can say for whatever that is." He gestured to her wrap.

"Fashion requires suffering," she replied, though her chattering teeth undermined the bravado.

They began walking east, falling into step together. The storefronts they passed were shuttered and dark, snowbanks piled against brick walls, streetlamps casting pools of yellow light at regular intervals. Their footsteps crunched in perfect synchronicity against the salt-crusted sidewalk.

"I almost didn't come out tonight," Lily admitted, watching her breath bloom white in the darkness. "It was easier to stay home. Safer."

"You sure you don't want to call it?" he asked, voice soft again. "We could bail, get a Lyft, I'll make sure you get home in one piece."

She thought about it. The prospect of her bed, of unspooling tonight alone with a mug of chamomile, was genuinely tempting. But it felt like a surrender, and she wasn't ready for that. Not with Devon beside her, not with the city still humming and the air so sharp it made her feel awake for the first time in days.

"No," she said finally. "I want to walk. Is that okay?"

He nodded, gave her arm a reassuring squeeze. "That's more than okay."

They passed shuttered bodegas and the skeletal trees that lined the avenue. The streetlamps cast their odd, sodium glow, turning every patch of snow a color somewhere between orange and rust. A pair of cops idled by the curb in their cruiser, watching the nightlife wind down. Devon kept his head up, scanning the horizon as if they were on a mission, while Lily watched the city's surface for hazards. They moved together with a kind of practiced choreography, each anticipating the other's shifts in pace and direction.

After a block, she felt the conversation pick itself up again, like a thread tugged back into her hand.

"Did you ever think it would be like this?" she said, gesturing at the city, the club, the night.

He glanced down at her, searching her face for context. "You mean... us?"

She shook her head, letting a lock of hair fall into her eyes. "No, just—being out. Being who we are, I guess. It still feels weird, sometimes." She felt the urge to apologize for her clumsiness, to explain that she didn't mean to go heavy, but Devon only seemed to listen harder.

He took a moment, considering. "Sometimes I feel like the city is a suit I'm wearing. Some nights it fits better than others. But it's always mine, you know?"

She let that roll around for a moment. The city as a suit—a costume, but one you owned, could alter and wear into the ground. She liked that. She could work with that.

At the end of the block, Lily stopped abruptly. The crosswalk signal flashed a red hand, though not a single car disturbed the empty intersection. The streetlights cast long shadows across the pavement, transforming ordinary cracks into mysterious hieroglyphics that disappeared beneath the crusted snow.

"What's wrong?" Devon asked, his voice cutting through the silence.

A shiver worked its way up Lily's spine, settling between her shoulder blades. She couldn't explain why she'd stopped—something about the emptiness ahead, the decision point of the corner, the way the night seemed to hold its breath. Before she could answer, Devon moved closer until their shoulders touched, his warmth seeping through the layers of their coats.

"Nothing," she said finally. "Just... taking it all in."

Devon didn't push away or pull her forward. He simply stood beside her, their breath mingling in the frigid air. In that stillness, Lily became acutely aware of the precise points where their bodies connected—shoulder to shoulder, the brush of his sleeve against hers, the way his height made him a perfect windbreak against the January chill.

The moment stretched, elastic and unhurried. No words, just the synchronization of their breathing and the distant hum of the city. Lily felt something settle in her chest, a quiet certainty that hadn't been there before.

When the light changed, they stepped off the curb together. Lily's heel caught momentarily in a crack, making her wobble.

"Those shoes," Devon said, steadying her with a hand at her elbow, "are a genuine health hazard. You know they make these amazing things called boots? With flat soles? And insulation?"

Lily rolled her eyes, but couldn't suppress her smile. "And deny myself the pleasure of tottering around like a newborn giraffe? Never."

"Your commitment to suffering for fashion is truly inspirational," Devon laughed, his eyes crinkling at the corners.

They reached the opposite curb, and Lily noticed a warm glow bleeding into the night ahead. Just ahead, the Starlight Diner pulsed with neon life—pink and blue tubes outlining its wide windows and spelling out its name in cursive against the dark. The light caught in the crystalline edges of snowbanks, transforming them into cotton candy sculptures.

"There it is," Devon said, nodding toward the diner. "Echo's recommendation. Think the coffee's really as good as she claims?"

Lily hesitated, suddenly aware of how the night was shifting. The diner meant extending this—whatever this was—beyond the protective bubble of The Glass Heel.

It meant sitting across from Devon under fluorescent lights, no music to fill awkward silences, no darkened corners to hide insecurities.

"Only one way to find out," she said finally, the words coming out more confident than she felt.

Chapter 5

The Starlight Diner

The neon sign's electric hum called to them like a beacon in the night, casting alternating washes of cherry-red and powder-blue across Lily's face as they approached the diner's entrance. Devon stepped ahead to pull open the heavy glass door, a rush of warm air scented with coffee and butter escaping into the frigid night.

"After you," he said, his voice soft against the January chill.

Lily stepped inside, the sudden warmth making her cheeks tingle as blood rushed back to her frozen skin. The Starlight Diner unfolded before her—a time capsule of chrome and vinyl that gleamed under fluorescent lights. Conversations hummed around her, punctuated by the occasional clink of silverware against ceramic and the sizzle of something delicious on the grill behind the counter.

A waitress with silver-streaked hair piled into a loose bun looked up from wiping down the counter. Her name tag—Gloria—caught the light as she nodded toward the half-empty restaurant. "Seat yourselves, honey. Anywhere you like."

Devon's hand found the small of Lily's back, a gentle pressure guiding her past a table of nurses still in scrubs, their laughter carrying the slightly manic edge of people coming off a twelve-hour shift. In the corner booth, a trucker with a salt-and-pepper beard nursed a mug of coffee while flipping through a dog-eared paperback. Two booths down, a woman with kohl-smudged eyes stared into the middle distance, her fingers absently tracing patterns in spilled sugar.

"This okay?" Devon asked, gesturing to an empty booth by the window. The vinyl was cracked in places, patched with silver duct tape that had yellowed at the edges.

Lily nodded, sliding onto the bench seat. The vinyl squeaked beneath her as she settled in, her silk dress whispering against the worn material. Devon took the seat opposite her, his broad shoulders filling the narrow space. The table between them felt smaller than she'd expected, their knees almost touching beneath it.

Gloria appeared beside them, coffee pot in one hand, menus tucked under her arm. "Coffee?" she asked, already setting down two white mugs with practiced efficiency.

"Please," Devon said, smiling up at her. The waitress filled both mugs with coffee the color of mahogany, steam rising in delicate spirals that carried the rich aroma of fresh brew.

"Are you serving breakfast yet?" Lily asked, suddenly aware of a hollow feeling in her stomach. The bourbon from earlier had faded, leaving behind a pleasant warmth and unexpected hunger.

"Honey, we serve breakfast twenty-four hours a day," Gloria said, her voice carrying the slight rasp of someone who'd been talking—or perhaps smoking—for decades. "It's our specialty." She set the laminated menus in front of them. "Take your time. I'll be back to take your order when you're ready."

Lily studied the menu, the laminated pages sticky against her fingertips. The offerings were comfortingly predictable—a diner classic with pages of breakfast options followed by sandwiches and blue plate specials. Her stomach growled as she scanned the egg section, suddenly realizing how hungry she was after hours of dancing.

"The pancakes look good," Devon said, his menu already closed and pushed to the side. He'd made his decision with the quick efficiency she was beginning to recognize as characteristic of him. No waffling, no second-guessing.

"Scrambled eggs and bacon for me," Lily decided, closing her own menu. She glanced up to find Devon watching her, a small smile playing at the corners of his mouth. "What?"

"Nothing. Just... this is nice. Normal." He gestured around the diner with its chipped mugs and flickering fluorescent light. "Different from the club."

Gloria appeared before Lily could respond, order pad in hand. "Ready, dears?"

They placed their orders—Devon's stack of pancakes with a side of sausage, Lily's eggs and bacon—and handed over the menus. As Gloria walked away, Lily wrapped her hands around her coffee mug, letting the warmth seep into her palms.

"So," Devon said, "corporate paralegal. What's that really like?"

Lily reached for the metal creamer pitcher, pouring a generous stream into her coffee until it turned the color of caramel. She tore open one sugar packet, then another, then a third, emptying each with methodical precision before stirring until the spoon clinked rhythmically against the ceramic. Only after the first sip, now sweet and milky against her tongue, did she answer.

"It's... complicated. On paper, it's perfect. Good benefits, decent salary, respectable title." Her finger traced the rim of her mug, collecting a drop of cream. "But there are days when I feel like I'm invisible. I do all this work—important work—and it's like I'm a ghost."

"What do you mean?" Devon leaned forward, his forearms resting on the table between them.

"Last month, I saved a partner's ass on a major contract review. Found a clause buried in the fine print that would have cost our client millions." She shook her head, remembering the hours spent poring over documents, the eye strain, the missed dinner plans. "When he presented to the client, he took all the credit. Didn't even mention my name."

Devon's brow furrowed. "That's messed up."

"That's corporate law." Lily shrugged, trying to make the gesture casual even as the familiar frustration tightened her chest. "I'm good at what I do—really good. But it's like they've decided what box I fit in, and they can't see beyond it."

"I get that," Devon said, nodding slowly. "The box

thing."

"Yeah?"

He took a long sip of his coffee before setting the mug down with deliberate care. "In construction, there's this... assumption. First time I walk onto a site, I see it in their faces." His jaw tightened slightly. "They look at me and I can see the calculations running behind their eyes. They think, 'This guy's too short to handle the heavy lifting.' Or they figure I can't possibly understand structural engineering at my size." He gave a short laugh, but there was no humor in it. "Like somehow being under six feet tall means my brain is smaller too."

Lily nodded, recognizing the frustration in his voice. "What do you do?"

"I work twice as hard. Lift twice as much. Know twice as much about load-bearing calculations and material tolerances." He shrugged, but the casualness of the gesture couldn't hide the tension in his shoulders. "I've deadlifted guys a foot taller than me who were struggling with support beams. I've drawn up plans that saved historic buildings the tall guys said couldn't be saved."

His calloused fingers curled around his coffee mug, knuckles whitening slightly. "But the best part? The absolute best part of what I do is standing in a finished space—something I helped create—and knowing it wouldn't exist without me. That building will be there long after all of us are gone. That's... that's something real, you know?"

The passion in his voice made something flutter in Lily's chest. She watched as his face transformed, the frustration melting away to reveal a quiet pride that softened the lines around his eyes.

"I'd love to see one of your buildings sometime," she said, surprising herself with the sincerity of the offer.

Devon's eyes met hers, a smile spreading slowly across his face. "Yeah? The theater renovation should be done in a few weeks. Opening night gala and everything. Maybe—"

Gloria appeared with their food, plates steaming in the cool diner air. She set Devon's stack of pancakes in front of him—golden discs dripping with melting butter and maple syrup—and Lily's eggs and bacon before her, the eggs fluffy and the bacon perfectly crisp.

"Anything else I can get you two?" Gloria asked, already backing away toward another table that needed attention.

"We're good, thanks," Devon said, picking up his fork with obvious anticipation.

They fell into comfortable silence as they ate, the diner's ambient noise—the clink of silverware, the hiss of the grill, the murmur of late-night conversations—filling the space between them. Lily watched Devon cut into his pancakes with methodical precision, creating perfect triangular bites that he consumed with obvious enjoyment. There was something endearing about his unabashed appreciation for simple pleasures.

"Good?" she asked, nodding toward his plate.

"So good," he confirmed around a mouthful of pancake. "Want to try?"

Before she could answer, he'd already cut a perfect bite and was offering it across the table on his fork. The gesture was intimate in its casualness, as if they'd shared meals a hundred times before. Lily hesitated only briefly before leaning forward to accept the bite, her lips parting to take the bite. The fork slid between her lips, and she wrapped her mouth around it, savoring the warm, buttery sweetness. As she pulled back, her eyes met his, and for a moment, the diner around them seemed to fade away.

"It's good," she said after swallowing, "but a little too sweet for my taste."

Devon smiled, setting his fork down. "Sweet tooth's one of my few vices. That and collecting vinyl records I rarely listen to."

"You have syrup," he said suddenly, gesturing toward her face. "Right there on your lip."

Lily felt a flush creep up her neck. She dabbed at her mouth with her fingertip, missing the spot entirely. "Did I get it?"

"No, it's—" Devon hesitated, then leaned forward across the table. Without thinking, he reached out and gently swiped his thumb across her bottom lip, removing the drop of maple syrup. His touch was warm and slightly rough against her skin, lingering just a heartbeat longer than necessary.

Time seemed to suspend itself. Lily felt her breath catch in her throat, her pulse quickening beneath her skin. Devon's eyes widened slightly, as if he too was surprised by his own boldness. The fluorescent lights hummed overhead, casting shadows across the planes of his face.

"I'm sorry," he said, pulling his hand back quickly. "That was... I shouldn't have—"

"It's okay," Lily interrupted, her voice softer than she'd intended. The spot where his thumb had touched her lip still tingled, a ghost of sensation that lingered like an echo. "Really."

Devon's shoulders relaxed, the tension melting away as he settled back against the booth. "I tend to be too direct sometimes. Occupational hazard. In construction, there's not much room for subtlety."

Lily smiled, finding his honesty refreshing. "I spend my days with people who take five paragraphs to say what could be said in five words. Direct is... nice."

The moment passed, but something had shifted between them. The air felt charged, like the atmosphere before a summer storm. Lily took another sip of her coffee, using the moment to collect herself. The diner continued its late-night rhythm around them—Gloria refilling mugs, the cook calling out orders, the bell above the door jingling as a group of college students stumbled in from the cold.

"So, vinyl records?" she asked, steering them back to safer ground. "What kind of music?"

Devon's face lit up, his passion evident. "Mostly jazz and blues. Some classic rock. I found this original pressing of Miles Davis's 'Kind of Blue' at a garage sale in Pilsen last summer. Guy selling it had no idea what it was worth."

"I actually played piano growing up," Lily admitted, setting down her fork. "Started when I was seven. My parents thought it would make me more well-rounded."

Devon's eyebrows raised. "Seriously? You never mentioned that before."

"It's not something I usually bring up. I was good, though. Really good." She traced a pattern in the condensation on her water glass. "I used to play Chopin nocturnes when I couldn't sleep. There was something about those melancholy arpeggios that just... made sense to me."

"You still play?"

Lily shook her head. "I haven't touched a piano in years. Not since before my transition." The word hung between them, released into the air of the diner like a bird uncertain of its flight path.

Devon's expression didn't change. He simply nodded, waiting for her to continue if she wanted to.

"It's strange," she said, her voice dropping lower. "Music was this thing that was just mine, you know? Not tied to gender or expectations. But somehow after I started transitioning, I couldn't bring myself to sit at the bench. Like I was afraid it would feel different, and I couldn't bear it if it did."

"Do you miss it?" Devon asked.

"Every day." She looked up at him, studying his face. "What about you? Any musical talents hidden under all that construction knowledge?"

Devon laughed. "I'm strictly a listener. But I've got a decent singing voice in the shower."

Their laughter mingled in the space between them, warm and easy. Lily felt something loosen in her chest—a tightness she hadn't realized she'd been carrying all night.

"When did you know?" she asked suddenly. "That you needed to transition?"

The question surprised even her. It wasn't something she typically discussed with anyone, let alone someone she'd just met. But something about Devon's steady presence made the words tumble out before she could catch them.

Devon didn't hesitate. "I was twelve. Standing in front of my bedroom mirror, and it just... clicked. Like

I'd been looking at a puzzle with the pieces forced into the wrong places, and suddenly I could see how they were supposed to fit." He took a sip of his coffee. "Took another five years to tell anyone, though."

"Twelve is young to have that clarity," Lily said.

"What about you?"

She twisted her napkin in her lap. "Later. Twenty-two. I spent a lot of years thinking I was just... wrong somehow. That I needed to try harder to be the person everyone saw." Her throat tightened. "Some days I still feel that way."

"The dysphoria never really goes away completely, does it?" Devon's voice was gentle.

"No," Lily admitted, feeling a strange relief at saying it aloud. "I have days when I look in the mirror and all I can see are the things that feel wrong. My hands are too big. My voice still feels too deep sometimes, especially when I'm tired." The confession spilled out of her before she could censor it. Lily looked down at her half-eaten eggs, suddenly vulnerable beneath the harsh diner lights. "I've done everything—the hormones, the voice training, the careful way I move through the world—but there are still moments when I look in the mirror and see him staring back at me."

Devon didn't flinch or offer empty reassurances. Instead, he reached across the table and placed his hand over hers. His palm was warm, slightly calloused against her skin.

"I get that," he said, his voice low enough that only she could hear him. "I've been on T for fifteen years, had top surgery a decade ago, and there are still mornings I wake up and feel like an imposter in my own skin."

Lily looked up, meeting his steady gaze. "How do you handle it?"

Devon shrugged, a small, decisive movement. "I decided a long time ago that I couldn't care less what other people thought about me." He tapped his temple with his free hand. "What matters is in here. The rest is just noise."

"Just noise," Lily repeated, testing the words. "That sounds... liberating."

"It is. And it isn't." Devon's thumb traced a small circle on the back of her hand. "Takes work every day. But I figure, I've built entire buildings from the ground up. I can build myself too, brick by brick, exactly how I want to be."

The simplicity of his philosophy struck Lily with unexpected force. She'd spent so many years calculating each gesture, modulating her voice, second-guessing every choice—all to meet some invisible standard of womanhood she'd created in her mind. The thought of letting go of that exhausting vigilance felt both terrifying and exhilarating.

"I wish I could do that," she admitted. "Just... not care."

"You can," Devon said, his expression earnest. "It's a muscle you build over time. Gets stronger with use."

A comfortable silence fell between them, punctuated by the clink of forks against plates at neighboring tables and the soft hiss of coffee brewing. Gloria appeared with the pot, refilling their mugs without breaking their moment, her experienced movements a silent acknowledgment of the conversation's weight.

"Thank you," Lily said after Gloria had moved on,

"for not making it weird. Some guys get uncomfortable when I bring it up."

Devon's mouth quirked into a half-smile. "Those guys are missing out on knowing you. Their loss."

The simplicity of his statement made something warm unfurl in Lily's chest. She took a sip of her freshly poured coffee, letting its bitterness ground her in the moment. Outside the window, snow had begun to fall again—fat, lazy flakes drifting past the neon sign, catching its pink and blue glow before disappearing into the darkness.

Lily glanced at her watch and felt a jolt of surprise. The tiny gold hands pointed to just after four in the morning. How had time slipped away so quickly? The diner had become a sanctuary of sorts, their booth a private island amid the gentle clatter of the late-night crowd. Unlike the electric energy of The Glass Heel, with its pulsing lights and watchful eyes, here they'd found something quieter but no less potent. The harsh fluorescents should have been unflattering, should have broken whatever spell had begun in the club's indigo shadows, but instead, they'd revealed something more genuine—the fine lines at the corners of Devon's eyes when he smiled, the way his hands moved with precise intention as he spoke.

"Oh my god, it's after four," she said, turning her wrist to show him. "I have a client meeting at nine."

Devon leaned back against the cracked vinyl. "I've got a site inspection at eight." He didn't sound particularly concerned, just stating a fact. His gaze remained steady on her face.

The thought of sitting through a three-hour contract review on no sleep made Lily's head throb. She imagined herself nodding off while a junior partner droned on about liability clauses, her makeup smudged from the night before.

"I think I need to call in," she admitted, the decision crystallizing as she spoke it. "There's no way I'll be functional."

Devon nodded, pulling his phone from his pocket. "Same. My crew can handle the inspection without me for one day."

They made their calls simultaneously—Lily leaving a carefully worded voicemail about a migraine for her firm's office manager, Devon texting his foreman with simple instructions. The small act felt oddly intimate, like they were co-conspirators in a minor rebellion against their daytime selves.

When she set her phone down, Lily felt a curious lightness. She couldn't remember the last time she'd called off work for anything other than actual illness. Certainly never for something as frivolous as staying up all night talking with someone who'd been a stranger just hours ago.

"So," Devon said, sliding his phone back into his pocket, "what now? Dawn's coming soon."

The question hung between them, weighted with possibility. Lily traced the rim of her coffee mug, considering. The sensible answer would be to thank him for a lovely evening, catch a rideshare home, and collapse into her own bed. That's what the carefully constructed version of herself—the one who color-coded her calendar and never missed a deadline—would do.

But the version of herself who'd walked into The Glass Heel tonight, who'd danced in Devon's arms and shared confidences over diner coffee, wanted something else.

"You could come back to my place," she said, the words emerging with surprising steadiness. "If you want to."

Devon's expression remained carefully neutral, but she caught the slight widening of his eyes, the subtle way his breath caught. He set his mug down, his calloused fingers lingering on the warm ceramic.

"Are you sure?" he asked, his voice low enough that only she could hear it. No pressure in his tone, just gentle consideration.

Lily felt her heart quicken, but her resolve didn't waver. This wasn't like her—she never invited men she'd just met back to her home. But Devon wasn't just anyone. The hours they'd spent talking had created something between them that felt both new and familiar, like finding a path she'd somehow always known was there.

"I'm sure," she said, meeting his gaze directly. "I'm not ready for tonight to end."

A smile spread across his face, reaching his eyes and softening the lines at their corners. "Neither am I."

Devon raised his hand, catching Gloria's attention with a small wave. "Check, please?"

As Gloria tallied their bill, Lily gathered her wrap and clutch, suddenly aware of the butterflies in her stomach. She wasn't proposing anything beyond conversation—at least, she didn't think she was—but the invitation still felt significant, a boundary crossed.

Devon reached for the check before she could, sliding it toward him with quiet determination.

"I can split it," Lily offered, already reaching for her

purse.

"Please," Devon said, his voice gentle but firm. "Let me get this one."

She recognized the same quiet certainty she'd seen in him all night—the confidence that came from knowing exactly who he was and what he wanted. Lily nodded, letting her hand fall away from her clutch.

They made their way to the register near the front door, Devon's hand finding the small of her back again, his touch light through the silk of her dress. The warmth of his palm seeped through the thin fabric, a contrast to the chill she could already feel emanating from the glass doors ahead.

Devon handed his credit card to Gloria, who ran it through with practiced efficiency. As they waited, Lily glanced around the diner one last time—at the nurses finishing their meal, the trucker now dozing over his empty coffee cup, the cook visible through the service window, flipping pancakes with mechanical precision. The Starlight Diner had become another milestone in whatever was unfolding between them, as significant in its fluorescent ordinariness as The Glass Heel had been in its velvet mystery.

"All set," Gloria said, handing back the card and receipt. "You two take care now."

The blast of cold air hit Lily like a physical blow as Devon pushed open the door. The temperature had dropped further, the wind whipping between buildings with renewed viciousness. Her silk wrap offered virtually no protection against the biting cold, and she felt goosebumps rise immediately along her bare arms.

"Oh god." Lily wrapped her arms around herself, the silk of her dress like tissue paper against the brutal wind. "It's like standing in a freezer."

Devon moved closer, positioning himself between her and the wind. "Let me flag down a cab."

The street was nearly deserted, the occasional car passing without slowing. Lily's teeth chattered uncontrollably now, her body shivering so hard she could barely stand straight. Each gust of wind cut through her wrap like it wasn't even there, freezing the sweat that had dried on her skin beneath her dress.

"There!" Lily thrust her arm out suddenly, spotting the yellow glow of a taxi turning onto their street. She stepped toward the curb, her heels wobbling on the icy sidewalk, and waved frantically. The cab's headlights swept over them as it pulled to the curb, its tires crunching through dirty snow.

Devon pulled open the back door, and blessed heat poured out into the night. "After you," he said, his voice nearly lost in another howl of wind.

Lily didn't need to be told twice. She slid across the cracked leather seat, the warmth of the cab's interior making her frozen skin tingle painfully. Devon followed, closing the door against the bitter cold, his large frame filling the space beside her.

"Milwaukee and Lawrence, please," Lily said, watching the driver's Cubs cap bob in the rearview mirror. He pulled away from the curb without a word. The taxi's heater wheezed to life, pumping out air that tasted of artificial pine and someone else's cigarette break, but after the knife-edge cold outside, it felt like salvation. Lily stretched her hands toward the vent, her fingertips tingling painfully as they began to thaw.

Chapter 6

Jefferson Park

The taxi lurched forward, swallowing them into its yellow sanctuary as Chicago's winter night pressed against the windows. Lily watched the Starlight Diner recede in the rearview mirror, its neon sign growing smaller until it was just a crimson smudge against the darkness, like a memory already fading.

The silence between them hummed with possibility. Devon sat close enough that she could feel the warmth radiating from his body, his thigh nearly touching hers on the cracked leather seat. The driver navigated through empty streets, the cab's heater wheezing asthmatically as it struggled against the January chill.

"Are you allergic to dogs?" Lily blurted, the question tumbling out before she could reconsider. It seemed absurdly practical after the night they'd shared, but suddenly vital to know.

Devon turned to her, the passing streetlights casting alternating shadows across his face. "No, why?"

"I have a dog. A Papillon named Poppy." Lily twisted her fingers in her lap. "She's tiny but thinks she's a Great Dane. Very protective."

"I like dogs." His smile creased the corners of his eyes. "They're better judges of character than most people."

Lily nodded, picturing Poppy's reaction to this man—her delicate ears perked forward in assessment, her tail either a blur of welcome or stiff with suspicion. "She'll probably bark at you for exactly forty-seven seconds, then demand you scratch behind her ears."

"Sounds fair. I respect a dog with standards."

The cab turned north, moving deeper into residential neighborhoods. Lily watched the cityscape transform—buildings growing shorter, streets wider, the sidewalks emptier. She'd made this journey countless times, but tonight it felt like crossing some invisible border, bringing Devon from his world into hers.

"I should warn you," she said, her voice softer now, "my place is pretty modest. Nothing special." She paused, remembering the subtle markers of wealth she'd grown up with but tried to distance herself from. "Not like my parents' house in Park Ridge."

Devon's eyebrows lifted slightly. "Park Ridge? That's... nice area."

The understatement made her wince. Park Ridge meant sprawling Tudor-style homes with manicured lawns, country club memberships, and garages that housed more cars than people.

"I grew up there, but it never felt like me," Lily

admitted. "Too many expectations. Too much... performance." She glanced at him. "What about you? Where's home?"

"Auburn Gresham," Devon said, his voice carrying a note of quiet pride. "Born and raised. Still live there."

Lily blinked, recalibrating. Auburn Gresham—predominantly Black, working class, miles from both The Glass Heel and her North Side neighborhood. A community with deep roots but faced with disinvestment and the lingering effects of redlining. She felt a flush of embarrassment heat her cheeks. She'd never considered where Devon might live—had pictured him in a trendy loft downtown, maybe, or a rehabbed apartment in Wicker Park. The realization that she'd unconsciously assumed so much about him made her stomach twist with discomfort.

"My whole family's still there," Devon continued, seeming not to notice her reaction. "My mom, two sisters, nieces and nephews all within a few blocks. Been offered management positions that would let me move somewhere fancier, but..." He shrugged, a simple gesture that conveyed volumes. "Those roots matter to me."

Lily nodded, uncertain what to say. The distance between Park Ridge and Auburn Gresham wasn't just geographic—it represented worlds of difference in opportunity, resources, and experience that she'd taken for granted.

"I like that," she said finally. "The closeness. Having people who know your history."

The cab turned onto her street, a quiet row of modest townhomes with small, manicured front yards. Most windows were dark at this hour, though a few early risers had lights glowing behind curtains. The driver pulled to a stop in front of her building, the meter's red numbers glowing in the darkness.

"This is me," Lily said, reaching for her purse. She pulled out her wallet before Devon could protest and handed the driver enough cash to cover the fare plus a generous tip. "My invitation, my treat."

Devon's expression softened, the beginning of an argument dying on his lips. "Thank you."

They stepped out into the cold, the cab's taillights receding down the quiet street. Lily led the way up the short path to her front door, her heels clicking against the concrete. The small porch light illuminated their breath, visible puffs of white in the frigid air.

At the door, Lily opened her clutch, fingers fumbling through lipstick, phone, and tissues. "My keys are in here somewhere," she muttered, the cold making her fingers clumsy. "I swear I put them in the inside pocket..."

Devon waited patiently, hands in his pockets, his solid presence beside her somehow both calming and nerve-wracking. Finally, her fingers closed around the familiar metal. "Got them!"

The key slid into the lock with a satisfying click. Lily pushed the door open and reached for the light switch, flooding the entryway with warm light. Her townhome revealed itself—neat and orderly, with bookshelves lining the living room walls, filled with carefully organized volumes. A plush gray sofa faced a modest television, while a small dining table occupied the space near the kitchen doorway. Everything in its place, just as she preferred it.

Before she could say anything, a blur of white and caramel fur came skittering across the hardwood floors, nails clicking rapidly as it approached. Poppy, all four pounds of her, planted herself between them, tiny paws planted firmly on the floor as she unleashed a volley of high-pitched barks. Her triangular ears stood at full alert, and her feathered tail whipped back and forth in a blur of motion.

"Poppy, it's okay," Lily said, kneeling down to scoop up the indignant ball of fluff. The dog continued her tirade from the safety of Lily's arms, her small body vibrating with each bark. "This is Devon. He's a friend."

Devon chuckled, his broad shoulders relaxing as he extended a hand toward the dog. "Hello there, fierce guardian. Nice to meet you."

Poppy sniffed his fingers suspiciously, her barking gradually subsiding into curious whimpers. After exactly forty-six seconds—one shy of Lily's prediction—the dog's entire demeanor transformed. Her tail began to wag furiously, and she strained toward Devon with unmistakable interest.

"I think she likes you," Lily said, surprised by the quick turnaround. Poppy was usually more discerning with strangers.

"Dogs can sense good people," Devon replied, gently scratching behind Poppy's ears. The tiny dog practically melted at his touch, her eyes closing in bliss.

Lily set Poppy down, and the dog immediately began dancing around Devon's feet, jumping up on her hind legs and spinning in joyful circles. The sight of her tiny guardian so thoroughly charmed broke the nervous tension that had been building since they'd left the cab.

"Would you like something to drink?" Lily asked, slipping off her heels with a sigh of relief. Her feet ached after hours of dancing, and the cool hardwood felt heavenly against her soles.

"That would be great, thanks."

Lily padded into the kitchen, Poppy trailing after her with occasional glances back at Devon to ensure he was still there. She opened the refrigerator door, the light illuminating her face as she surveyed the contents.

"Let's see... I've got sparkling water, orange juice, almond milk..." She pushed aside a container of leftover Thai food. "Or wine, if you'd prefer something stronger."

"Just water is perfect," Devon called from where he stood examining her bookshelves. "Nothing fancy."

Lily pulled two Fiji water bottles from the refrigerator, the rigid plastic cool and unyielding in her palm as condensation beaded against her fingertips. When she returned, Devon stood before her bookshelves, head tilted slightly as his index finger hovered over the spines.

"You've got these arranged by author," he said, eyes moving methodically across the shelves.

"Actually—" Lily handed him one of the bottles, their fingers brushing momentarily, "I've got them by genre first, then author. Classics on the top shelf, contemporary fiction below, reference books at the bottom."

"Impressive organization," Devon said, following her to the gray sofa. He settled into one corner while she took the other, Poppy immediately jumping up to wedge herself between them. He twisted the cap off his water and took a sip, then gestured with the bottle. "When I said 'nothing fancy,' I was expecting tap water in a plastic cup. This is practically luxury."

Lily laughed, the sound softer in the quiet of her home than it had been in the diner. "Sorry to disappoint.

I can pour it into a mug if that would make you feel better."

"No, this is perfect." His smile reached his eyes, crinkling the corners in a way that made her chest tighten.

A comfortable silence settled between them. Lily tucked her feet beneath her, the silk of her dress cool against her skin. The late hour—or early, depending on perspective—created a strange bubble around them, as if they existed in a pocket of time separate from the rest of the world.

"You have a beautiful home," Devon said, his gaze traveling around the room. "It feels... peaceful."

"Thank you." Lily absently stroked Poppy's fur. "I needed a sanctuary after everything. Somewhere that was just mine, you know?"

Devon nodded, his expression softening. "After my transition, I felt that way too. Needed a space where every object was chosen by me, for me. No history. No expectations."

"Exactly." Lily's throat tightened with unexpected emotion. "My parents' house was full of... ghosts. Pictures of someone who didn't exist anymore. Clothes in closets that never fit right. Trophies with the wrong name."

She hadn't meant to be so honest, but something about the gentle darkness of pre-dawn, the safety of her own space, and Devon's attentive presence broke down barriers she usually maintained.

"What was hardest for you?" she asked, surprising herself with the directness of the question. "After you transitioned?"

Devon took another sip of water, his gaze thoughtful. "The relationships. Some people couldn't make the leap—they kept looking for the person they thought they knew." His fingers tapped a gentle rhythm against the water bottle. "My dad left. Just... couldn't handle it. Said he'd lost his daughter."

"I'm sorry," Lily whispered.

"It hurt like hell at the time," Devon admitted. "But my mom was incredible. She said she hadn't lost anyone—she'd just gained a better understanding of her child." A small smile touched his lips. "She started buying me men's clothes before I even asked."

"My parents..." Lily's voice caught, and she had to swallow hard before continuing. "They never officially disowned me. Not like your father did. But sometimes I think that would have been cleaner, you know? A clean break."

Poppy sensed the shift in Lily's energy and curled closer against her thigh. Lily ran her fingers through the dog's silky fur, anchoring herself.

"They still call me by my deadname," she continued, the words scraping her throat raw. "My mother sent a birthday card last month addressed to... to him. After seven years of hormone therapy, after legally changing my name, after everything."

Devon's face remained steady, his eyes never leaving hers. He didn't rush to fill the silence with platitudes or solutions, just created space for her words to exist.

"The worst part is the way they pretend. Like if they just wait long enough, this phase will pass." Lily's laugh held no humor. "My father still introduces me as his son when I visit. Seven years, and I don't think they've ever once called me Lily."

The admission hung in the air between them. Saying it aloud made the pain tangible in a way it hadn't been before, even to herself. Her chest tightened, a physical ache spreading beneath her ribs.

"What about tonight?" Devon asked softly. "At The Glass Heel. When Echo knew your name. When Julian saw you. When we danced."

Something broke inside Lily then, like a dam giving way after years of pressure. Tears welled in her eyes, blurring Devon's face into a warm smudge across from her.

"They saw me," she whispered, her voice cracking. "Not who I'm trying to be, not who I was before, just... me. Lily." The first tear spilled over, tracking a warm path down her cheek. "God, do you know how rare that is?"

Devon moved closer, careful not to disturb Poppy. His hand found hers on the couch between them, calloused fingers wrapping around her softer ones.

"I do know," he said. "It's why I keep going back."

The gentleness in his voice undid her completely. Lily's shoulders shook as the tears came faster now, seven years of contained grief finding its release. She tried to turn away, embarrassed by the breakdown, but Devon's hand tightened around hers.

"Hey," he said, his voice low and steady. "It's okay. You don't have to hide this from me."

Poppy whimpered and jumped down from the couch, circling anxiously at their feet. Through her tears, Lily felt the cushion shift as Devon moved closer. His arm wrapped around her shoulders, solid and warm, pulling her gently against him. She resisted for only a moment before letting herself collapse against his chest, her tears soaking into his shirt.

"I'm here," Devon whispered, his hand gently stroking her back. "Just let it out."

Lily surrendered to the comfort of his embrace, her body trembling with each sob. The warmth of his chest against her cheek anchored her as years of carefully contained grief poured out. His heart beat steady beneath her ear, a rhythmic reminder that she wasn't alone in this moment.

"It's okay," he murmured, his breath warm against her hair. "You're safe here."

Devon's arms remained solid around her, neither tightening with discomfort nor pulling away. He simply held her, his palm making slow circles between her shoulder blades. The faint scent of his cologne—sandalwood and something citrusy—mingled with the clean cotton smell of his shirt as she breathed in deeply, trying to steady herself.

"I never cry in front of people," she managed between shuddering breaths. "Never."

"Then I'm honored you trust me enough," Devon said, his voice a low rumble she felt through his chest.

His fingers found their way to her hair, gently stroking the soft strands. Lily felt his chin rest lightly on the top of her head as he drew in a deep breath, as if taking in the scent of her shampoo. The intimate gesture made her heart flutter despite her tears.

"You deserve to be seen, Lily," he whispered. "For exactly who you are."

The words washed over her like warm water,

dissolving another layer of her defenses. She closed her eyes, letting herself be held, letting herself be vulnerable in a way she hadn't allowed in years—perhaps ever.

When her tears finally began to subside, Lily pulled back slightly, suddenly self-conscious. Her makeup must be a disaster, mascara streaked down her cheeks, lipstick smudged beyond repair. She wiped at her face with trembling fingers.

"God, I must look terrible," she said, attempting a laugh that came out as a hiccup.

Devon's eyes met hers, warm and steady in the soft lamplight. "You look beautiful," he said simply.

Fresh tears welled in her eyes at the sincerity in his voice. One escaped, tracking down her cheek toward the corner of her mouth. Devon's gaze followed its path, and then his hand lifted, his thumb gently catching the tear before it reached her lips. The callused pad of his thumb was surprisingly soft against her skin, lingering a moment longer than necessary.

Time seemed to slow as his eyes dropped to her mouth, a question in their depths. Lily's breath caught in her throat, her heart hammering against her ribs. Devon leaned forward with exquisite slowness, giving her every chance to pull away.

She didn't.

His lips met hers with gentle pressure, warm and surprisingly soft. The kiss was tentative at first, a question asked and answered in the space between heartbeats. Lily's eyes fluttered close as his hand moved to cradle her cheek. The tenderness in his touch undid her completely. His kiss was a lifeline in a stormy sea, an anchor when she felt most adrift. She leaned into him, her hand finding the solid warmth of his chest, feeling his heartbeat quicken beneath her palm.

The kiss deepened, not with passion but with recognition—as though their lips were speaking a language their words couldn't quite capture. Devon's thumb stroked her cheek, wiping away the remnants of her tears. The salt of her sadness mingled with the sweetness of their connection, creating something entirely new between them.

When they finally parted, Devon rested his forehead against hers. Their breath mingled in the quiet space between them. Lily kept her eyes closed, savoring the moment, afraid that opening them might break whatever spell had wrapped around them in the predawn stillness of her living room.

"I've wanted to do that since I saw you at the bar," Devon whispered.

Lily opened her eyes to find him looking at her with such tender intensity that her breath caught. "I'm glad you waited until now," she said. "It means more here. Like this."

He nodded, understanding exactly what she meant. Here, in her sanctuary, with her makeup smeared and her defenses down, the connection between them felt authentic in a way it couldn't have at The Glass Heel.

Devon's hand moved to trace the line of her jaw, his touch reverent. "You're incredible, Lily," he said, his voice low and certain. "Everything about you."

She shook her head slightly, not in disagreement but in wonder at his words. His fingers drifted to the top button of his shirt, and he hesitated, a question in his eyes. Lily nodded, her heart racing as he began to undo each button with deliberate care.

The fabric parted to reveal his chest, and Lily's gaze

traveled over the smooth brown skin, taking in the neat scars that ran in twin curves beneath his pectoral muscles. They were paler than the rest of him, silvery in the soft light, telling a story of transformation and courage that resonated deep in her soul.

"Beautiful," she whispered, reaching out to touch him. Her fingertips traced the edge of one scar, feeling the slightly raised texture against his warm skin. Devon's breath hitched at her touch, his eyes never leaving her face.

"They used to bother me," he admitted. "Now they just remind me of how far I've come."

Lily nodded, understanding completely. Her own body carried different markers of her journey—some visible, others known only to her. She reached behind herself, finding the zipper of her dress with trembling fingers.

"Let me," Devon said softly.

She turned, offering her back to him. His fingers found the zipper with a delicacy that made her breath catch, the metal teeth parting with a whisper that raised goosebumps along her spine. The silk dress slid from her shoulders, hesitated at her waist, then surrendered to gravity in a hushed cascade. Standing in the gentle glow of the lamp, Lily felt both exposed and liberated. Her breasts—the result of a decision she'd made for herself, a careful choice that honored the body she wanted—caught the soft light. Her hands twitched at her sides, fighting the instinct to shield herself from his gaze.

Lily pivoted to meet his gaze. Devon's eyes found hers first, then drifted downward like gentle hands, lingering at each curve and hollow. His expression held none of the predatory assessment she'd braced herself for—instead, his face softened with something that looked almost like reverence, as though he were witnessing a rare and perfect moment he wanted to preserve forever.

"You're beautiful," he whispered, his voice rough with emotion.

Lily's breath caught in her throat. The words weren't empty flattery; they carried the weight of recognition. Of seeing and being seen. Her skin prickled with goosebumps that had nothing to do with the cool air.

She moved toward him, her heart pounding against her ribs. Devon opened his arms, and she stepped into his embrace, the warmth of his bare chest against her skin sending a wave of comfort through her body. His arms encircled her, strong and secure, creating a sanctuary of touch.

"Is this okay?" he asked, his breath warm against her hair.

"More than okay," she murmured, tilting her face up to his.

Their lips met again, and this time the kiss deepened, slow and tender. Devon's hand cradled the back of her head, his fingers tangling in her hair as he pulled her closer. The world narrowed to the points where they connected—lips, hands, skin against skin. Time stretched and compressed, minutes bleeding into each other as they explored this new intimacy.

They sank back onto the couch together, Lily curling against Devon's side. His arm wrapped around her shoulders, his fingers tracing idle patterns on her skin. The weight of the day—of their unexpected connection—settled over them like a warm blanket.

"I should go put something on," Lily murmured,

though she made no move to leave the circle of his arms.

"You don't need to," Devon said. He reached for the throw blanket folded over the arm of the sofa and draped it over them both. "Unless you're uncomfortable."

"I'm not," she admitted, surprised by the truth of it. "This feels... right."

Devon's eyes found hers in the soft lamplight, a question lingering in their amber depths. Lily answered by leaning forward, her lips meeting his with newfound certainty. This kiss felt different—unhurried and deep, as if they had all the time in the world. His hand cupped her cheek, thumb tracing the delicate line of her jaw as her fingers threaded through his hair, holding him close.

"I never expected this," she whispered against his lips. "When I walked into The Glass Heel tonight..."

"I know," he murmured, his voice a low rumble that vibrated against her skin. "Me neither."

They shifted on the sofa, finding a more comfortable position with her head nestled against his chest, his arm wrapped securely around her shoulders. The blanket cocooned them in shared warmth, creating a world of just the two of them. Poppy had settled into a tight ball at the far end of the couch, her tiny snores punctuating the comfortable silence.

Lily traced the edge of Devon's scar with gentle fingertips, feeling the slightly raised tissue beneath her touch. "Thank you," she said softly.

"For what?"

"For seeing me. Really seeing me."

Devon pressed a kiss to her forehead, his lips warm

against her skin. "Thank you for letting me."

The first hints of dawn began to filter through the blinds, painting thin stripes of pale gold across the floor. Outside, a cardinal announced the morning with its bright, insistent call. Lily felt her eyelids growing heavy, the emotional and physical exhaustion of the night finally catching up with her.

Devon's breathing had already deepened, his chest rising and falling in a steady rhythm beneath her cheek. His arm remained protectively around her, even as sleep began to claim him. Lily smiled, allowing herself to sink into the comfort of his embrace.

"Sleep well," she whispered, though she wasn't sure if he could hear her.

His only response was to pull her closer, a small, unconscious gesture of protection that made her heart swell. Lily's eyes grew heavy, then closed completely as her breathing slowed to match his. Devon followed moments later, his fingers still curled possessively around her shoulder even as sleep claimed him. Just as they both surrendered to dreams, the morning light crept across the hardwood, transforming dust motes into floating gold, illuminating two people who had been searching in the dark until, finally, they'd found each other.

Chapter 7

A Day of Their Own

Lily woke to sunlight striping her face and Devon's arm heavy across her waist. For a moment, disorientation clouded her thoughts—why was she on the couch instead of in bed?—before memories of the night before crystallized. The Glass Heel. The diner. Devon.

She blinked against the brightness, squinting at the wall clock. Almost noon. Her body felt stiff from sleeping on the sofa, her neck protesting as she tried to shift without waking Devon. His breathing remained steady, warm against her shoulder, his body radiating heat that had kept her comfortable through the night despite the lack of blankets.

A small whine from the floor drew her attention. Poppy sat at attention, triangular ears perked forward, dark eyes fixed on Lily with unmistakable urgency.

"I know," Lily whispered. "Bathroom time."

The movement of extracting herself from Devon's embrace proved more complicated than anticipated. His arm tightened reflexively as she began to slide away, pulling her closer against the solid warmth of his chest. Lily paused, savoring the sensation for a moment before placing her hand over his.

"Devon," she murmured. "I need to get up."

His eyes opened slowly, confusion giving way to recognition as he focused on her face. A smile spread across his features, crinkling the corners of his eyes.

"Morning," he said, his voice rough with sleep. "Or is it afternoon?"

"Almost noon." Lily gestured toward Poppy, who had begun pacing in tight circles. "Someone needs to go out."

Devon released her immediately, running a hand over his face as he sat up. "Sorry."

"Don't apologize." Lily rose from the couch, goosebumps rising on her exposed skin. Last night flooded back—her breakdown, his tenderness, clothes discarded between kisses that tasted of salt and need. She crossed her arms over her chest, suddenly self-conscious.

Devon's gaze remained fixed above her collarbone, the deliberate restraint making her pulse quicken. "I should get going. Give you back your day."

"Stay," Lily said, surprising herself with how much she meant it. She tucked a strand of hair behind her ear. "We've both already called out. We could just... have today. Together."

Devon's expression softened, surprise giving way to

something that looked almost like relief. "I'd like that. A lot."

"Good." Lily smiled, feeling suddenly lighter. "Let me take Poppy out and then we can figure out the rest."

She slipped into her bedroom to pull on yoga pants and an oversized sweater, then clipped the leash to Poppy's collar. The tiny dog pranced in excited circles, her nails clicking across the hardwood floors as she led the way to the back door.

"I'll be right back," she called over her shoulder.

The brisk morning air rushed against her face as she stepped onto her small patio. Poppy trotted across the frost-dusted grass, sniffing intently at each blade before finding the perfect spot. Lily hugged her arms around herself, the thin sweater doing little against the January chill. The events of last night replayed in her mind—her vulnerability, Devon's gentle acceptance, the way his lips had felt against hers. Her cheeks warmed despite the cold.

When Poppy finished, Lily led her back inside, the warmth of the townhouse enveloping her like a blanket. She found Devon in the living room, his button-up shirt now covering his chest, the fabric stretching across his compact frame as he bent to retrieve his socks from beside the couch. The sight of him moving comfortably through her space sent a flutter through her stomach.

"Hey," he said, looking up with a smile that reached his eyes. "That was quick."

"Poppy's not a fan of the cold either." Lily unclipped the leash, and the tiny dog immediately scampered toward Devon, dancing around his feet with her tail wagging furiously.

Devon crouched to scratch behind Poppy's ears,

his fingers finding exactly the right spot. "Smart dog." He straightened. "So, I'm actually starving. Would it be okay if I ordered us some takeout? My treat."

"I was thinking we could make something instead," Lily suggested, the idea forming as she spoke it. "I have pasta, and there's homemade sauce in the fridge. We could do pasta with garlic bread?"

Devon's face lit up. "That sounds amazing. I haven't had a home-cooked meal in weeks."

"Don't get too excited. The sauce is pre-made," Lily admitted with a laugh. "But it's good—my own recipe."

They moved to the kitchen together, Poppy trailing behind them like a tiny supervisor. Lily pulled a pot from the cabinet and filled it with water, setting it on the stove to boil. The refrigerator door opened with a soft whoosh as she retrieved a glass container of deep red sauce.

"This needs garlic, onions, and some fresh herbs," she said, setting the container on the counter. "Think you can handle that part?"

Devon rolled up his sleeves, revealing the corded muscles of his forearms. "I think I can manage. Where's your cutting board?"

"Second drawer on the left," Lily directed, reaching for the pasta in the pantry. She watched as Devon moved through her kitchen with unexpected confidence, finding a knife and setting up his workspace with practiced efficiency.

"You seem at home in a kitchen," she observed, measuring out the pasta.

Devon shrugged, his knife making quick, precise cuts through the garlic. "My mom insisted all her kids learn to cook. Said it was the one skill that would keep us alive when everything else failed."

"Smart woman," Lily said, adding salt to the now-bubbling water before dropping in the pasta.

The kitchen filled with the earthy scent of garlic as Devon worked, his hands moving with the same confidence she'd noticed on the dance floor. He glanced up, catching her watching him.

"What? Am I doing it wrong?"

"No, just..." Lily smiled, stirring the pasta. "You look like you know what you're doing."

"Unlike on the dance floor?" His eyebrow arched playfully.

"I never said that." Heat crept up her neck as she remembered the way he'd held her, how their bodies had fit together.

Devon grinned, dicing an onion with quick efficiency. "You're blushing."

"It's the steam from the pasta," she protested, turning back to the pot.

They worked in comfortable synchronicity, moving around each other in the small kitchen space with an ease that surprised Lily. When Devon's arm brushed against hers as he reached for the olive oil, she felt the contact like a current through her skin.

"So this famous sauce of yours," Devon said, scraping the chopped garlic and onions into a small bowl. "Family recipe?"

Lily shook her head. "Self-taught through trial and error. My mother's idea of cooking was calling her personal chef."

Devon whistled low. "Fancy. And yet here you are,

making your own sauce."

"Rebellion takes many forms," she said with a wry smile. "Mine just happens to involve excessive amounts of basil."

Devon laughed, the sound warming the space between them. "I like that. Culinary rebellion."

Lily checked the pasta, fishing out a strand to test its doneness. "Almost there." She glanced over at Devon, who was now chopping fresh basil, the herb's sweet scent filling the air. "Could you grab the garlic bread? It's in the freezer, bottom drawer."

"On it." Devon moved to the freezer, pulling out a foil-wrapped loaf. "Oven temperature?"

"Four hundred. There should be a baking sheet in the cabinet next to the stove."

As Devon prepared the garlic bread, Lily opened another cabinet and took out two plates, the ceramic cool against her fingertips. She gathered silverware from the drawer and carried everything to the small dining room table, arranging them carefully.

The timer for the pasta beeped just as Devon slid the garlic bread into the oven.

"Perfect timing," he said, setting the oven timer for eight minutes.

Lily drained the pasta in a colander, steam rising in a fragrant cloud that dampened her face. She returned the pasta to the pot and poured in her sauce, adding Devon's freshly chopped ingredients. The rich aroma of tomatoes, garlic, and basil filled the kitchen as she stirred everything together, the wooden spoon making soft scraping sounds against the bottom of the pot.

"That smells incredible," Devon said, leaning over

her shoulder to inhale deeply.

When the garlic bread was golden and fragrant, Devon pulled it from the oven with a dish towel wrapped around his hand. He sliced it into thick pieces that released clouds of buttery steam, the scent mingling with the pasta sauce in a mouthwatering combination.

"Let's just eat right here," Lily suggested, gesturing to the kitchen counter. "Seems silly to get fancy after sleeping on the couch all night."

Devon nodded, his smile warm. "I like the way you think."

They served themselves banquet style, spooning the pasta directly from the pot onto their plates and adding slices of garlic bread from the baking sheet. Their shoulders brushed as they moved around each other, a casual intimacy that sent pleasant shivers across Lily's skin. She reached into the refrigerator and pulled out two more bottles of Fuji water, their sides already beading with condensation.

"Here," she said, handing one to Devon. Their fingers touched during the exchange, lingering a moment longer than necessary.

They carried their food to the small dining table, settling across from each other. Steam rose from the pasta in delicate spirals, carrying the rich scent of herbs and garlic. Lily twirled her fork in the pasta, suddenly aware of Devon's eyes on her. She glanced up to find him watching her with an expression that made her heart skip.

"What?" she asked, heat rising to her cheeks.

"Nothing," he said, but his eyes didn't leave her face. "Just... I like seeing you in your space. You seem different here. More yourself."

Lily ducked her head, focusing on her plate. "Is that good or bad?"

"Definitely good." Devon took a bite of pasta, his eyes closing briefly as he savored it. "This sauce is amazing, by the way."

"Thanks," she murmured, pleased by the compliment.

They ate in companionable silence for several minutes, the only sounds the soft clink of forks against plates and Poppy's occasional snuffling as she circled hopefully beneath the table. Lily found herself sneaking glances at Devon between bites, studying the way his hands moved, how his shoulders filled out his rumpled shirt, the subtle dimple that appeared in his right cheek when he smiled.

Each time she looked up, she found his eyes already on her, his gaze steady and unabashed. Unlike her furtive glances, Devon watched her openly, a slight smile playing at the corners of his mouth. The directness of his attention made her both self-conscious and exhilarated.

"You keep looking at me," she said finally, breaking the silence.

"You keep looking at me too," he countered. "The difference is I'm not hiding it." He took another bite of pasta, his gaze never wavering.

Heat spread across Lily's cheeks. She ducked her head, focusing intently on twirling pasta around her fork. "I'm not used to being watched like this."

"Like what?" Devon's voice was soft, curious.

"Like I'm... interesting." The admission fell from her lips before she could stop it.

Devon set down his fork. "You are interesting."

Lily glanced up, caught in his amber gaze. Words seemed unnecessary in that moment. His eyes tracked the curve of her cheek, the way her hair fell across her forehead, how her fingers curled around her water bottle. She felt both exposed and cherished under his attention.

The silence stretched between them, filled with unspoken thoughts. Lily found herself cataloging the details of him—the slight stubble darkening his jaw, the way his collar lay open at his throat, the precise strength in his hands as he broke off another piece of garlic bread.

She let her guard down, allowing herself to really look at him without the self-consciousness that usually made her glance away. Devon met her gaze steadily, a small smile playing at the corners of his mouth. He didn't fill the silence with idle chatter or nervous questions, just let the moment breathe between them.

When they finished eating, Lily rose from her seat, gathering their empty plates. "I should wash these."

Devon nodded, standing as well. "I'll help."

At the sink, Lily turned on the water, adjusting the temperature until steam rose in delicate wisps. She squirted dish soap onto a sponge, creating a small mountain of bubbles that smelled of artificial lemons. Devon appeared at her side, dish towel in hand.

"I'll dry," he offered, his shoulder brushing against hers in the narrow space before the sink.

Lily nodded, handing him the first clean plate. Their fingers touched beneath the ceramic, warm skin against cool porcelain. She pointed toward a cabinet to her right. "Plates go in there."

Devon moved to open the cabinet door, his elbow bumping against her shoulder as he reached across her. Water splashed onto her sweater.

"Sorry," they said in unison, then laughed.

Devon attempted a different approach, shifting behind her to access the cabinet, but his foot found Poppy instead, who let out an indignant yelp.

"Sorry, girl," he said, startling backward and bumping against Lily's hip. The plate tilted dangerously in his grasp.

A laugh escaped Lily, genuine and unguarded. "We need some kitchen choreography here."

"I'll just stack them over here for now," Devon said, gesturing to the countertop. "Less chance of canine casualties."

Lily nodded, grateful for the simple solution. They fell into an easy rhythm—her washing, him drying and stacking—that required no words, just the occasional brush of hands as dishes passed between them. The quiet domesticity of the task settled around her like a comfortable blanket. She couldn't remember the last time she'd shared something this mundane with another person.

When the last fork was dried and set aside, Lily wiped her hands on a dish towel and leaned against the counter. The afternoon stretched before them, open and unstructured.

"Do you want to watch a movie?" she asked, the suggestion coming naturally, as if they spent Saturdays like this all the time. "I've got pretty much every streaming service."

Devon's face brightened. "That sounds perfect."

He tapped his fingers against his jaw, considering. "Have you seen 'The Seventh Seal'? Bergman classic, black and white, guy literally plays chess with Death."

Lily blinked, trying to hide her surprise. "Um, can't say that I have."

"Or 'Stalker'? Tarkovsky? Three-hour Russian masterpiece about a journey through a mysterious zone?"

She shook her head, a smile tugging at her lips. "I was thinking more along the lines of 'The Proposal' or 'When Harry Met Sally.'"

Devon clutched his heart in mock horror. "Rom-coms? Really?"

"Says the man who just suggested I spend my Friday off watching a Russian art film." Lily crossed her arms, unable to suppress her grin. "I bet you're one of those people who pretends to understand French New Wave cinema."

"I'll have you know I genuinely enjoy Godard," Devon said with exaggerated dignity, then cracked a smile. "But I'm not above a good rom-com. How about a compromise? 'Eternal Sunshine of the Spotless Mind'? Romance with a sci-fi twist."

Lily considered this. "I've actually never seen it. Is it good?"

"One of my favorites," Devon said, his expression softening. "Weird but beautiful. Kind of like..." He paused, looking at her with an intensity that made her breath catch. "Kind of like this thing between us."

Heat rushed to her face. "Okay, you've convinced me."

Lily grabbed her remote from the coffee table and

navigated to Amazon Prime. She searched for the title, her heart speeding up when it actually appeared on screen.

"Would you look at that," she said, pointing the remote at the screen where the movie thumbnail appeared. "Prime has it. Just four bucks to rent."

"Fate," Devon replied with a smile that made her stomach flutter.

She clicked the 'rent' button without hesitation, the small purchase feeling somehow significant. The screen loaded with the film's moody thumbnail image while Lily set the remote down.

"I should probably make this more comfortable," she said, pushing herself up from the couch. "Do you want anything to drink? I could make some popcorn too."

Devon patted his stomach. "I'm still pretty full from lunch, thanks. That pasta was filling."

"We definitely need a blanket though." Lily gestured toward the stairs. "I've got a really soft one in the linen closet upstairs. I'll just be a second."

She took the stairs quickly, her sock feet silent against the wood. The upstairs hallway felt cooler, removed from the warmth of Devon's presence. She opened the narrow door of her linen closet and reached for her favorite throw—a plush microfiber blanket in a deep forest green that was large enough to cover two people comfortably.

When she returned downstairs, Devon had settled more deeply into the couch, one arm stretched along its back. He looked so at home there, as if he belonged in her space. The thought sent a pleasant shiver through her.

"Perfect timing," he said as she approached. "I just finished reading the description."

Lily unfolded the blanket with a flourish and settled back onto the couch beside him. Without awkwardness or hesitation, Devon lifted his arm in invitation. She scooted closer until their sides pressed together, the solid warmth of him radiating through her sweater. He draped his arm around her shoulders as she spread the blanket over both their laps.

"Cozy?" he asked, his voice soft near her ear.

"Very," she replied, letting herself relax against him.

She pressed play, and the film's opening scene filled the screen. The blanket trapped their shared body heat beneath it, creating a pocket of warmth that made Lily feel both protected and thrillingly aware of every point where their bodies connected—hip to hip, her shoulder against his chest, his arm a gentle weight across her shoulders.

As the story unfolded, Lily found herself drawn into its strange, melancholy world. The character of Joel reminded her of people she'd known—quiet men with rich inner lives that few bothered to discover. She felt Devon's reactions through his body—the slight tensing during uncomfortable moments, the rumble of laughter she could feel through his chest when something amusing happened.

"Oh, that's brutal," she whispered when Joel discovered Clementine had erased him from her memory. Devon's arm tightened around her shoulders, a silent acknowledgment of her reaction. The film pulled them both in, its exploration of memory and love unfolding in fragments that somehow made perfect sense.

Lily sank deeper into the cushions, her body melting against Devon's as the story progressed. His chest rose and fell in a steady rhythm beneath her cheek, his heartbeat a comforting percussion she could feel through his shirt. The blanket cocooned them, soft and warm, creating an intimate bubble that separated them from the rest of the world.

She found herself mirroring Devon's reactions throughout the film—gasping when he tensed, laughing when he chuckled, her body somehow attuned to his without conscious thought. When Joel and Clementine tried desperately to hide in Joel's childhood memories, Lily felt Devon's fingers tighten slightly on her shoulder, the gesture communicating more than words could.

"That's incredible," she whispered during a particularly poignant scene, tilting her face up to catch his expression. Devon looked over at her, their faces suddenly close, his eyes reflecting the flickering light from the screen.

"Yeah," he murmured, though she wasn't sure if he was agreeing about the film or acknowledging something else entirely. His gaze lingered on her face for a moment before returning to the screen, but his arm pulled her fractionally closer, his thumb tracing small circles against her sweater.

The afternoon light shifted as they watched, golden rays slanting through the blinds and painting stripes across the floor. Poppy had settled at their feet, her tiny body curled into a perfect circle of fur, occasional doggy dreams making her paws twitch. Lily found herself less focused on the film and more aware of Devon—the subtle scent of his cologne mingled with the fabric softener from his shirt, the solid warmth of his thigh pressed against hers under the blanket, the way his chest expanded with each breath.

When the credits finally began to roll, accompanied by Beck's melancholy guitar, neither of them moved immediately. The spell of the film lingered, wrapping around them like another layer of the blanket they shared. Lily felt a curious tightness in her chest, a mixture of the film's bittersweet ending and her awareness of Devon beside her.

"What did you think?" Devon asked, his voice low and slightly rough, as if he hadn't used it in hours.

Lily shifted to look up at him, suddenly aware of how close their faces were. "It was beautiful," she said. "Sad but hopeful somehow."

"Worth the $3.99?" His eyes crinkled at the corners, the teasing question carrying a deeper meaning she couldn't quite articulate.

"Definitely," she replied, her voice softer than she'd intended. "Best four dollars I've spent in a long time."

Devon's smile faded slowly, his expression growing more serious as his eyes traveled over her face. Something shifted in the air between them, the comfortable warmth shifting into something more heated as his gaze dropped to her lips.

Lily felt her heart quicken, her breath catching in her throat as Devon leaned forward, closing the small distance between them. His lips met hers with gentle pressure that quickly deepened as she responded, her hand finding the solid warmth of his chest. Unlike their first kiss—tentative and comforting—this one ignited immediately, a spark catching dry tinder.

Devon's hand slid to her waist, fingers pressing into the soft fabric of her sweater as he pulled her closer. Lily shifted, turning to face him fully, her knee bumping against his thigh beneath the blanket. The kiss intensified, his tongue tracing the seam of her lips until she opened to him with a soft sigh that surprised even her.

Her fingers sank into his close-cut afro, the tight coils soft and springy against her skin as she held him to her. The movie's credits continued to scroll, forgotten, as Devon's other hand found her hip, his deep brown fingers contrasting against her pale sweater, guiding her until she was nearly in his lap, the blanket sliding unnoticed to the floor. His kiss was confident but unhurried, exploring her mouth with a thoroughness that made her toes curl inside her socks.

The gentle scrape of his stubble against her chin sent shivers racing down her spine. She pressed closer, wanting more of him, more of this delicious heat building between them. Devon's hand slid beneath the hem of her sweater, his palm warm against the small of her back, fingers splaying wide as if trying to touch as much of her as possible.

Lily gasped against his mouth as his thumb traced slow circles just above the waistband of her yoga pants. The sensation was electric, sending currents of pleasure radiating outward. Devon took advantage of her parted lips to deepen the kiss further, a low sound of appreciation rumbling in his chest that she felt more than heard.

The tentative sweetness of their earlier connection had transformed into something hungrier, more urgent. Lily's hands moved to the buttons of his shirt, fumbling slightly as she tried to undo them without breaking their kiss. Devon helped, his fingers brushing against hers as together they opened his shirt, revealing the warm brown skin and defined muscles beneath.

Her palms flattened against his chest, feeling the rapid beat of his heart, the smooth texture of his scars beneath her fingertips. Devon broke the kiss to look at her, his amber eyes dark with desire, pupils dilated in the afternoon light.

"You're beautiful," he whispered, his voice rough with want.

Lily surged forward, recapturing his mouth, no longer willing to waste time with words when she could be tasting him instead. His hands gripped her hips, lifting her fully onto his lap until she straddled him, her knees sinking into the couch cushions on either side of his thighs. The position brought them flush against each other, and she felt his arousal pressing against her core through the thin fabric of her yoga pants.

The pressure of him against her core sent a surge of heat through her body. She broke the kiss, panting slightly, and pressed her forehead against his. Their breath mingled in the narrow space between them, hot and quick.

"I think," Lily whispered, her voice husky with desire, "we should go upstairs. To my bedroom."

Devon's eyes darkened further, his hands tightening on her hips. "Yes," he breathed, the single word heavy with promise.

She climbed off his lap, her legs unsteady beneath her. Devon stood immediately, his shirt hanging open, revealing the smooth planes of his chest. He reached for her hand, his fingers interlacing with hers as if they'd done this a hundred times before. The simple connection sent another wave of heat through her body.

They moved toward the stairs, Lily leading the way, her heart pounding so loudly she was certain he could hear it. At the bottom step, Devon pulled her back against him, his lips finding the sensitive spot where her neck met her shoulder. She gasped, her knees nearly buckling as his teeth grazed her skin.

"Sorry," he murmured against her neck, not sounding sorry at all. "Couldn't wait."

Lily turned in his arms, her hand finding his cheek. "Then don't."

They stumbled up the stairs together, pausing every few steps when the need to touch became too overwhelming. On the landing, Devon pressed her against the wall, his mouth hot and demanding against hers. Lily's fingers sank into his close-cropped curls, holding him close as his hands slipped beneath her sweater, his deep brown palms warm against her ribs, thumbs brushing the undersides of her breasts.

A breathless laugh escaped her when they nearly tripped over the last step. Devon steadied her, his own laughter joining hers, the sound rich and warm in the hallway. The moment of lightness did nothing to diminish the heat between them—if anything, it made the connection feel more real, more intimate.

"Which door?" Devon asked, his voice rough with desire.

"End of the hall," Lily replied, already tugging him in that direction.

Chapter 8

Nothing Between

The last trace of restraint between them dissolved. Devon pulled her toward the bed, his hands firm on her hips as they moved in tandem. Their lips never separated, hungry and searching, breathing each other's air. Lily's fingers traced the muscles of his abdomen, feeling them tighten beneath her touch. Her back hit the edge of the mattress, and they tumbled down together onto the cool blue comforter.

A soft giggle escaped her lips as they bounced slightly on the mattress. Devon grinned down at her, his eyes crinkling at the corners, warm and intent. The afternoon light caught the amber flecks in his irises, turning them to liquid gold.

"Come here," she whispered, tugging at the open sides of his shirt.

He shrugged it off in one fluid motion, tossing it carelessly to the floor. Lily raised her arms as Devon's hands found the hem of her sweater, pulling it up and over her head in a single movement that left her hair slightly mussed. Her skin prickled in the cool air, goosebumps rising along her arms.

Devon's gaze traveled over her, taking in the pale blue lace of her bra, the gentle curves of her body. His expression made her feel beautiful, desired in a way that reached beyond the physical.

"You're incredible," he murmured, his voice rough with want.

He lowered himself to her, the warmth of his bare chest against hers sending waves of heat through her body. His hands moved up her sides, hesitating for just a moment before cupping her breasts. The gentle weight of his palms made her arch into his touch, seeking more pressure, more connection.

Devon's lips found her neck, pressing heated kisses along the sensitive skin. Lily's head fell back, giving him better access as his mouth moved lower, tracing her collarbone with his tongue. Each kiss left a trail of fire in its wake, her skin tingling where his lips had been.

He continued his downward path, pressing his mouth to the swell of her breast above the lace edge of her bra. Lily's breath caught in her throat as his fingers gently pushed the fabric aside, exposing her left nipple to the cool air. Devon's eyes met hers for a moment, seeking permission, and she nodded, unable to form words.

The warm heat of his mouth closed around her nipple, and Lily moaned softly, her back arching off the bed. His tongue circled the sensitive peak as his hand continued to caress her other breast through the thin lace. The dual sensation sent sparks of pleasure racing down her spine, pooling low in her belly.

"Devon," she breathed, her fingers sinking into the dense, springy curls of his close-cropped afro, the tight coils soft against her palms as she held him against her.

He hummed against her skin, the vibration adding another layer to the pleasure building within her. His free hand skimmed down her side, finding the waistband of her yoga pants. Lily lifted her hips in silent invitation. His fingertips hooked into the waistband of her yoga pants, and with gentle pressure, he slid them down her thighs. The soft fabric whispered against her skin as he revealed her matching lacy bikini briefs. Devon's breath caught as his gaze traveled over her, taking in the gentle curve of her hips, the slight bulge beneath the delicate lace. His eyes flicked up to meet hers, filled with nothing but warmth and desire.

Lily felt her heart hammering against her ribs as Devon's fingers traced the edge of her panties, his touch feather-light against her skin. She watched his face carefully, searching for any hesitation, any change in his expression, but found only reverence in his gaze.

His fingers slipped beneath the waistband of her underwear, pausing for a moment as his eyes sought hers again, asking a silent question. Lily nodded, lifting her hips slightly to help as he slowly pulled the lacy fabric down her legs.

As her body was revealed to him fully, Lily reached behind herself and unhooked her bra with trembling fingers. The straps slid down her shoulders as she pulled it away, exposing her breasts to the cool air of the bedroom.

Devon went still, his gaze traveling over her body with an intensity that made her skin warm beneath the late afternoon light. The sun through the blinds painted golden stripes across her nakedness—highlighting a hip here, the hollow of her throat there—as his eyes moved from her face to her breasts, down to her stomach, lingering with tender curiosity on her penis resting soft between her thighs. When his eyes returned to hers, they held such open wonder that Lily felt her throat tighten, unexpected tears threatening at the corners of her eyes.

"I've never seen anyone as beautiful as you," he murmured, his hand hovering just above her skin as if he were afraid she might break beneath his touch.

Lily reached for his hand, guiding it to her hip. "Touch me," she whispered. "Please."

Devon's palm was warm against her skin, his touch gentle but sure as his hand slid up her side, tracing the curve of her waist, the gentle swell of her breast. His thumb brushed across her nipple, and she gasped at the sensation, arching slightly into his touch.

His voice vibrated through her skin like distant thunder. "Tell me if you want me to stop.

She answered by pulling him closer, her fingertips pressing into the warm skin of his shoulders. "Don't you dare," she whispered against his ear.

Devon lowered himself beside her, one arm sliding beneath her shoulders as he pulled her close. His lips found hers in a kiss that started gentle but quickly deepened, his tongue sliding against hers as his hand continued to explore her body. His palm skimmed over her stomach, fingers trailing patterns across her skin that left goosebumps in their wake.

Lily's hands moved to his belt, fumbling slightly with the buckle. "Too many clothes," she murmured against his lips.

Devon smiled against her mouth, pulling back just enough to help her. Together, they worked his belt free, then the button and zipper of his jeans. Together they pushed his jeans down his muscular thighs. Devon kicked them off with a practiced motion, revealing a pair of black boxer briefs that hugged his compact frame. Lily's eyes traveled over the subtle bulge, her heartbeat quickening as she reached forward. Her fingertips hovered at the elastic waistband, slipping just beneath the edge, the warmth of his skin radiating against her touch.

She looked up, meeting his gaze. "May I?"

Devon's smile was gentle, his eyes darkening with desire as he nodded.

Lily slowly pulled the boxer briefs down, revealing a sleek harness with a soft silicone packer nestled in its center. She smiled, a warmth spreading through her chest that had nothing to do with physical desire and everything to do with recognition—of him, of herself, of the beautiful complexity they shared.

Devon reached down, adjusting the packer with practiced movements, positioning it until it stood erect between them. The transformation was both intimate and playful, and Lily couldn't help the soft giggle that escaped her lips.

His eyebrow quirked upward. "Something funny?"

"I'm sorry," she said, her smile widening. "It's just... it's cute. The way you did that."

Devon shook his head, but his eyes crinkled with amusement. "Cute, huh?" His palm connected with her hip in a gentle, playful slap. "Turn around for me."

His words made her tremble with anticipation. Lily repositioned herself, the mattress cool against her palms and knees as she turned away from him. Behind her, Devon's weight shifted the bed. The tear of a foil packet broke the silence. She gasped softly when the cold lubricant touched her skin, trickling between her cheeks. Devon's thumb moved in slow, deliberate circles, spreading the slickness while his other hand held her steady. She felt the pressure of the silicone against her, neither too firm nor too soft, as Devon's fingertips drew gentle patterns across her lower back, silently reassuring her.

She felt the silicone press against her entrance, firm but yielding. Devon's fingers traced gentle circles at the small of her back, soothing and arousing all at once.

"Is this okay?" he murmured, his voice low and rough.

"Yes," she breathed, pushing back slightly against him.

Devon pressed forward with exquisite slowness, the initial resistance giving way to a fullness that made Lily gasp. Her fingers curled into the comforter, bunching the fabric as pleasure bloomed through her body.

"You okay?" Devon's voice was strained, his fingers tightening on her hips.

"Don't stop," she whispered, the words catching in her throat as he pushed deeper.

The sensation was overwhelming—not just the physical fullness, but the trust it represented, the vulnerability they shared. Devon's hand slid around to caress her stomach, his touch grounding her as he began to move in slow, measured thrusts.

Lily closed her eyes, surrendering to the rhythm they created together. Each movement sent waves of pleasure cascading through her body, building toward something that felt both inevitable and miraculous.he sensation was overwhelming—not just the physical fullness, but the trust it represented, the vulnerability they shared. Devon's hand slid around to caress her stomach, his touch grounding her as he began to move in slow, measured thrusts.

Devon pumped in and out of her, finding a steady rhythm that made Lily's breath catch with each forward motion.

"Is it still cute?" he joked, his voice husky with exertion.

A laugh bubbled up from Lily's chest, surprising her with its lightness. "Definitely still cute," she teased, glancing back over her shoulder to catch his eye.

Devon's palm connected with her ass in a playful slap that sent an unexpected jolt of pleasure through her body. The sting bloomed into warmth that radiated outward, making her gasp.

"You can..." Lily hesitated, her voice dropping to a whisper as shyness momentarily overtook her. "You can go faster if you want."

Devon's fingers tightened on her hips, his thumbs pressing into the dimples at the small of her back. He quickened his pace, each thrust more insistent than the last. The new rhythm made Lily's arms tremble as she struggled to maintain her position, pleasure building at the base of her spine like electricity gathering before a storm.

"Like this?" Devon asked, his breathing ragged.

"Yes," Lily moaned, dropping down to her elbows as the new angle sent sparks of sensation coursing through her. "Just like that."

The blue comforter bunched beneath her fingers as she gripped it tightly, anchoring herself against the increasing intensity of Devon's movements. Sweat beaded along her hairline, trickling down her temple as her body flushed with heat. The afternoon sunlight caught the moisture on her skin, transforming ordinary perspiration into a golden sheen that highlighted the curve of her back, the slope of her shoulders.

Devon leaned forward, his chest warm against her spine as his lips found the nape of her neck. The gentle press of his mouth contrasted with the insistent rhythm of his hips, the contradiction sending shivers racing along her nerve endings. His hand slid beneath her, palm flat against her stomach, fingers dipping lower with clear intent.

"Is this okay?" he murmured against her ear, his fingers hovering just above where she ached for his touch.

"Please," was all Lily could manage, the word escaping on a shaky exhale.

His fingers found her, circling with perfect pressure that made her vision blur at the edges. The dual sensations—his hand and the steady thrusting—combined to create a pleasure so intense that Lily had to bite her lip to keep from crying out. Her body tensed, trembling on the precipice of release.

"Devon," she gasped, his name a prayer on her lips.

"I've got you," he whispered, his voice a caress against her skin. "Let go."

Lily surrendered to the sensations overtaking her body, a tidal wave crashing through every nerve ending. Her muscles tensed, then released in powerful waves as Devon's steady rhythm pushed her over the edge. She cried out, the sound echoing in the quiet bedroom as pleasure radiated from her core outward, leaving her trembling and gasping for breath.

Devon followed her over that precipice moments later, the base of the harness grinding perfectly against his swollen clit with each thrust. His movements became erratic as the pressure built, waves of pleasure radiating outward until his entire body tensed. A strangled groan escaped his throat as he stilled completely, forehead pressed against her shoulder blade, hips twitching with the aftershocks of his own release. His breath came in hot puffs against her sweat-dampened skin, chest heaving against her back.

For several heartbeats, they remained frozen in that position, connected and panting. Then Devon slowly withdrew, his hands gentle as he helped Lily turn onto her back. Her limbs felt like liquid, uncoordinated and heavy as she settled against the rumpled comforter. Devon stretched out beside her, propping himself on one elbow to look down at her flushed face.

"You're incredible," he murmured, tracing a finger along her collarbone.

Lily couldn't find words yet, her mind still hazy with aftershocks of pleasure. Instead, she reached up, pulling him down for a kiss that was soft and languid, their bodies cooling in the afternoon air.

When they finally broke apart, Devon eased the harness away from his body and moved from behind her with careful, deliberate movements. Lily's limbs trembled as she shifted from her position on elbows and knees, collapsing first onto her stomach before rolling languidly onto her back. Devon stretched out beside her, their shoulders touching, both of them breathing heavily. Lily stared at the ceiling, watching how the late afternoon light created shifting patterns as the breeze outside moved the branches near her window. Her body hummed with satisfaction, every muscle relaxed in a way she couldn't remember feeling before.

But the peaceful moment didn't last. Devon's hand found hers, squeezing gently before he sat up with renewed energy. His eyes were bright as he looked down at her, a mischievous smile playing at his lips.

"Round two?" he asked, his hand already sliding up her thigh.

Lily laughed, the sound surprised and delighted as she grabbed his wandering hand. "Already?"

"I've been thinking about this since I first saw you at The Glass Heel," Devon admitted, his fingers tracing idle patterns on her stomach. "One round isn't going to be enough."

Heat bloomed across Lily's skin at his words. She pushed herself up on her elbows, taking in the sight of him—his compact, muscular frame, the gentle curves of his scars, the hunger in his eyes that matched her own resurging desire.

"What did you have in mind?" she asked, her voice dropping to a husky whisper.

Devon shifted his weight, sliding the harness down his legs and setting it aside on the nightstand. His eyes never left Lily's face, watching the flush of arousal deepen her cheeks as he moved back toward her on the bed.

"I want to try something," he said, his voice low and rough with desire. He traced his fingertips along her thigh. "Would you be comfortable if we..." He hesitated, then moved to demonstrate rather than explain, turning his body around and positioning himself above her, his knees on either side of her head.

Lily felt her breath catch as she understood what he was suggesting. His thighs were muscular and strong on either side of her face, the soft folds of his vagina just inches from her mouth while he lowered his head toward her own arousal.

"Is this position okay for you?" Devon asked, his breath warm against her sensitive skin. "Are you comfortable giving me oral?"

Lily swallowed, a mixture of nervousness and excitement fluttering in her stomach. "I'm okay with it," she admitted, her voice barely above a whisper. "But I've never done oral on a vagina before."

Devon's laugh was gentle, without a trace of judgment. "And I've never done oral on a penis before," he said, shifting slightly to look back at her over his shoulder. "So this is going to be new for both of us."

The shared vulnerability in his admission made something warm bloom in Lily's chest. She reached up, her hands settling on his hips, guiding him closer.

"We'll figure it out together," she said, her confidence growing.

Devon lowered his head, his tongue tentatively tracing the length of her. The sensation made Lily gasp, her hips lifting involuntarily toward his mouth. Taking a deep breath, she leaned up, her tongue exploring the unfamiliar terrain of him with gentle curiosity

The taste was different than she'd expected—not unpleasant, just new. Salt and musk and something uniquely Devon. She followed his lead, mirroring his movements, learning what made his breath catch and his thighs tense around her head.

His own explorations grew bolder as his confidence increased, his hands holding her hips steady as he discovered what made her moan against him. The dual sensations—giving and receiving pleasure simultaneously—created a feedback loop that intensified everything. Each time she found a particularly sensitive spot that made Devon groan, the vibration of his voice sent shivers through her own body.

They established a rhythm together, her tongue exploring the wet folds of his vagina while his mouth worked over the sensitive head of her penis. Lily lost herself in the unfamiliar terrain of him—the soft ridges, the swollen bud of his clitoris that made him shudder when she circled it. Her earlier nervousness dissolved into wonder at how his body responded to her touch. Her hands gripped his thighs, feeling the muscles flex beneath her fingers as he pressed himself more firmly against her exploring mouth.

Devon's technique grew more confident with each passing minute, his tongue tracing the underside of her shaft before his lips encircled her, creating a pressure that made Lily's toes curl against the sheets. She tried to match his intensity, focusing on the swollen bud of his clitoris, circling it with her tongue the way she'd read about but never attempted.

When she applied gentle suction, Devon's thighs trembled around her head. She did it again, paying close attention to his reaction. A muffled groan vibrated against her own sensitive flesh, telling her she'd found something he liked. The sound sent ripples of pleasure through her body, encouraging her to continue.

They learned each other's bodies through this wordless conversation of gasps and shivers. Lily discovered that quick, light flicks of her tongue made

Devon press harder against her mouth, while Devon found that swirling his tongue around the head of her penis before taking her deeper made her hips buck upward involuntarily.

The afternoon sunlight painted golden stripes across their entwined bodies as they explored this new territory together. Lily lost herself in the rhythm they created, her world narrowing to the taste of him on her tongue and the exquisite sensations of his mouth on her. Every time she found a particularly sensitive spot, Devon would mirror the technique on her, creating an escalating spiral of pleasure.

Her fingers dug into the firm muscle of his thighs as tension began to build at the base of her spine. Devon's movements became more focused, more insistent, as if he sensed her approaching climax. His tongue swirled faster, his lips tightening around her as he took her deeper into his mouth.

Lily moaned against him, the vibration making his hips jerk. She redoubled her efforts, determined to bring him the same pleasure he was giving her. The taste of him grew stronger on her tongue as his arousal increased.

When the orgasm hit, it caught Lily by surprise. It rolled through her body in waves, starting at her core and radiating outward until even her fingertips tingled with sensation. She cried out against Devon's flesh, her hips lifting off the mattress as pleasure crashed over her.

The sound and movement must have pushed Devon over the edge as well. His thighs clamped around her head, his body trembling as he pressed himself against her mouth. She continued to move her tongue against him, gentler now, helping him ride out the aftershocks of his release.

For several long moments they remained frozen in that position, both catching their breath. Then Devon shifted, carefully moving off her and turning around to stretch out beside her on the rumpled comforter. His face was flushed, his eyes bright as he propped himself up on one elbow to look at her

"That was..." he began, then seemed to run out of words.

"Yeah," Lily agreed, her voice slightly hoarse. She stared up at the ceiling, suddenly shy about making eye contact despite the intimacy they'd just shared. She felt Devon's gaze on her face, warm and curious.

"That was..." Devon cleared his throat. "Different than I expected. In a good way."

Lily turned her head, meeting his eyes despite the heat rising in her cheeks. "Was it okay? I mean, I wasn't sure if I was doing it right."

"You couldn't tell?" Devon's eyebrows rose, a playful smile tugging at his lips. "Trust me, you did everything right."

Lily ducked her head, pleasure at his words mingling with lingering shyness. "I've never been with someone who... who understands. You know?" She gestured vaguely between their bodies, struggling to articulate the connection that went beyond physical.

Devon's expression softened. He reached out, brushing a strand of hair from her forehead with gentle fingers. "I know exactly what you mean. There's something about not having to explain or apologize for your body that's just..." He paused, searching for the right word. "Freeing."

"Yes," Lily whispered, relief washing through her at being understood so completely. "Freeing."

She traced idle patterns on the sheet between them, gathering courage for her next words. "I liked it. Being with you." The admission came out quieter than she'd intended, vulnerable in the golden afternoon light.

"I liked it too." Devon's voice carried no hesitation, just quiet certainty. "A lot, actually. You're amazing, Lily."

His directness made her smile even as she felt the flush deepen on her cheeks. Devon seemed so comfortable discussing intimacy, while she still felt the need to hide behind her hair, despite what they'd just shared.

"I never thought..." She paused, swallowed. "I never thought it could feel like that. So natural."

Devon's hand found hers on the sheet, his fingers sliding between hers with easy familiarity. "That's how it should feel. Like you're just being yourself."

Lily nodded, squeezing his hand. The air in the bedroom felt thick with possibilities, with words not yet spoken but hovering just out of reach. Her skin prickled with dried sweat, her hair tangled from their activities.

"I need to take a shower," she said suddenly, the practical thought breaking through the emotional haze.

Devon's fingers tightened briefly around hers. "Can I join you?"

Lily's heartbeat quickened at the suggestion, a warm rush spreading beneath her ribs. Instead of answering, she slid to the edge of the bed and stood, her legs still slightly unsteady, toes curling against the cool hardwood floor. She extended her hand, slender fingers wrapping around Devon's wrist where his pulse throbbed against her touch, and tugged gently.

He rose from the bed, the mattress springs creaking softly beneath his shifting weight, following her lead with a crooked smile that made her stomach flutter like trapped moths. She laced her fingers through his, feeling the slight calluses on his fingertips catch against her softer skin, the simple connection sending warmth through her palm and up her arm like honey-colored light as she led him toward the bathroom door with its peeling white paint.

Chapter 9

Out in the Open

Sunlight sliced through the blinds, painting golden stripes across Lily's bare shoulder. She stirred, consciousness returning in slow waves as the warmth touched her skin. Saturday morning. The realization settled over her with unexpected sweetness.

Beside her, Devon slept deeply, his breathing steady and even. One arm was still draped across her waist, his palm warm against her hip. Lily studied his face in the morning light—the gentle curve of his lips, the shadow of stubble darkening his jaw, the way his eyelashes rested against his cheeks. He looked younger in sleep, the usual alertness in his expression softened into something almost vulnerable.

Her stomach growled, the sound unexpectedly loud in the quiet bedroom. Lily pressed a hand against it, suddenly aware of how hungry she was. They hadn't eaten since the pasta yesterday afternoon, and her body was demanding sustenance after their night together.

As if hearing her thoughts, Devon's eyes fluttered open. He blinked twice, confusion giving way to recognition as his gaze found hers.

"Morning," he murmured, voice rough with sleep.

"Morning." Lily smiled, tucking a strand of hair behind her ear. "Sleep okay?"

Devon nodded, stretching his arms above his head. The sheet slipped down, revealing the smooth brown skin of his chest, the neat surgical scars catching the light. "Better than I have in months."

Her stomach growled again, louder this time. Heat rushed to Lily's cheeks as Devon's eyebrows rose, amusement crinkling the corners of his eyes.

"Hungry?" he asked, lips quirking into a smile.

"Starving, actually." Lily sat up, pulling the sheet with her. "I know this great pancake place nearby. They make these blueberry pancakes with lemon zest that are..." She closed her eyes, remembering the taste. "Incredible."

Devon propped himself up on one elbow, his expression warm. "Are you asking me on a breakfast date, Lily Warren?"

"I am." She leaned down, pressing a quick kiss to his lips. "What do you say?"

"I say yes to pancakes. Always." He caught her hand as she started to pull away, tugging her back for another kiss, this one slower, deeper. When they broke apart, Lily felt slightly breathless.

"Keep that up and we'll never make it to breakfast," she warned, though she couldn't keep the smile from her voice.

Devon released her with obvious reluctance. "Pancakes first. Then we'll see about dessert."

The promise in his voice sent a pleasant shiver down Lily's spine.

Forty-five minutes later, they stepped into Molly's Pancake House, a cozy establishment tucked between a hardware store and a dry cleaner. The bell above the door jingled as they entered, announcing their arrival to the half-full restaurant. The scent of coffee and maple syrup enveloped them as a hostess with a faded pink apron approached.

"Two?" she asked, already reaching for menus.

"Yes, please," Lily replied.

They followed the woman to a small booth by the window, sliding onto opposite benches. The vinyl seats squeaked beneath them, worn from years of use but clean and well-maintained. Morning light filtered through half-drawn blinds, casting a warm glow over the laminated menus the hostess placed before them.

"Coffee?" she asked, notepad already in hand.

"Please," they answered in unison, then glanced at each other with matching smiles.

When the hostess departed, Devon leaned forward, elbows on the table. "So, these legendary blueberry pancakes. Do they actually change lives, or was that just to get me out of bed?"

"Oh, they're life-changing," Lily assured him, her eyes dancing. "I discovered this place my first week in Jefferson Park. It was the only thing that made apartment hunting bearable."

Their coffee arrived in thick white mugs, steam

curling into the air between them. Lily reached for the small metal creamer, pouring a generous amount into her cup.

"Sweet tooth?" Devon asked, watching as she added three sugar packets.

"Only with coffee." She stirred carefully, the spoon clinking against ceramic. "Can't stand it bitter."

Devon took his black, wrapping his hands around the mug as if absorbing its warmth. "My dad used to say cream and sugar were for people who didn't actually like coffee."

"And what do you say?"

"I say drink what makes you happy." He took a sip, his eyes never leaving hers over the rim of his mug. "Life's too short for bad coffee."

A waitress appeared beside their table, pen poised over her order pad. "Ready to order?"

"Blueberry lemon pancakes," Lily said without opening her menu. "And a side of bacon, extra crispy."

"Make that two orders of the blueberry pancakes," Devon added. "But I'll take sausage links instead of bacon." He glanced at Lily. "Bacon's good, but sausage is superior at breakfast."

"Noted," she said with mock seriousness. "This could be a deal-breaker."

When the waitress left, Devon leaned back against the booth, his posture relaxed yet somehow still taking up space in a way Lily found fascinating. He moved with a confidence that never seemed to cross into arrogance.

"So, what's the strangest breakfast food you've ever eaten?" he asked, catching her off guard.

Lily laughed. "What kind of question is that?"

"The kind that tells you more about a person than asking about their job." His smile was playful. "Everyone has a weird food story."

"Hmm, I once ate chocolate-covered bacon at a state fair," Lily said, wrinkling her nose at the memory. "It was disturbing how not-terrible it was."

Devon laughed, the sound warm and rich. "That's barely strange. I was expecting pickled fish for breakfast or something truly bizarre."

"Fine, your turn then. Impress me with your breakfast adventures."

"Chicken feet soup," Devon said without hesitation. "My grandmother made it every Sunday morning. Black beans, chicken feet, and these little dumplings." His expression softened with the memory. "Took me until I was about twelve to appreciate it."

Their food arrived, steam rising from stacks of pancakes dotted with plump blueberries. The scent of lemon and warm butter filled the air between them. Lily watched as Devon cut into his stack with methodical precision, creating perfect triangular bites.

"You eat very... deliberately," she observed, pouring maple syrup in a spiral over her own pancakes.

Devon glanced up, fork paused midway to his mouth. "Construction habit. Everything has a process." He took the bite, his eyes closing briefly as he savored the flavor. "Okay, you weren't exaggerating. These are incredible."

Lily smiled, pleased by his reaction. "Told you."

They fell into comfortable conversation as they ate, discovering small details about each other that had been overlooked in the intensity of the previous day. Devon always saved the best bite for last. Lily couldn't stand when different foods touched on her plate. He drank his coffee in exactly four sips. She unconsciously hummed when something tasted good.

When they finished, Lily leaned back, feeling pleasantly full. "So, I was thinking... it's such a nice day. Have you ever been to the Garfield Park Conservatory?"

Devon shook his head. "Can't say that I have. Is it worth seeing?"

"It's beautiful—like stepping into another world. All these incredible plants from different climates, and the architecture is stunning." Lily tucked a strand of hair behind her ear. "We could go, if you want? It's not far on the Green Line."

"I'd like that," Devon said, his expression brightening. "I've lived in Chicago my whole life and never been. Seems like an oversight worth correcting."

The train swayed gently as it curved toward the Conservatory-Central Park Drive station. Lily watched the neighborhoods transform through the window—from the quiet residential streets of Jefferson Park to the busier commercial areas, finally emerging into the West Side with its distinctive character. Devon sat beside her, their shoulders touching, his presence solid and warm.

"This is us," she said as the automated voice announced their stop.

They stepped off the train into the crisp January air. The conservatory's glass dome gleamed in the distance, catching the winter sunlight. Lily pointed west. "There it is, just a half block that way."

They walked side by side, navigating the uneven

sidewalk. Tall bare trees lined the street, their branches etched against the bright blue sky. A light dusting of snow crunched beneath their feet.

"So you come here often?" Devon asked, his breath clouding in the cold.

"Not as much as I'd like," Lily admitted. "But whenever I need to remember there's more to the world than contract law and deadlines. Something about all that green life in the middle of winter... it helps me breathe."

Devon nodded, his eyes crinkling at the corners. "I get that. Sometimes on construction sites, I'll notice a plant growing through concrete or rebar. Always feels like a reminder."

"Of what?"

"That life finds a way, I guess. Even in the most unlikely places."

The Garfield Park Conservatory came into view, its glass dome gleaming in the sunlight. The historic structure rose from the landscape like a crystal palace, promising warmth and life within its walls.

"There it is," Lily said, unable to keep the excitement from her voice.

They approached the entrance, a modest doorway that belied the wonders inside. As they stepped into the lobby, Lily felt the first rush of humid air against her face, carrying the earthy scent of soil and greenery.

A small line had formed at the ticket counter. When they reached the front, the attendant smiled at them. "Two adults?"

"Yes, please," Lily said, already reaching for her wallet.

Devon started to protest, his hand moving toward his back pocket, but Lily shook her head. "My invitation, my treat. It's only twenty dollars."

"Are you sure?" His eyebrows raised slightly.

"Absolutely," she said, handing over her credit card before he could argue further.

The attendant processed the payment and handed them a small map. "Enjoy your visit."

They moved past the counter into the first chamber of the conservatory. The Palm House rose before them, a cathedral of glass and iron filled with towering trees that reached toward the distant ceiling. The temperature jumped at least thirty degrees, wrapping around Lily like a warm, damp blanket. She unbuttoned her coat, already feeling perspiration forming at her hairline.

"Wow," Devon breathed beside her, tilting his head back to take in the massive fronds overhead. "It's like stepping into another continent."

Lily slipped her coat off completely, draping it over her arm as the tropical warmth enveloped her. The air felt alive against her skin—thick and soupy, carrying the scent of earth and growth. Towering palms created a green canopy overhead, their massive fronds filtering the sunlight into dappled patterns that shifted across the walkway.

"It's like we've been transported to the Amazon," she said, her voice hushed with wonder.

Devon nodded, unbuttoning his own coat. "The engineering alone is incredible. Look at how they've created this perfect microclimate."

They wandered deeper into the Palm House, following the curving path that wound between giant trees. Their footsteps echoed slightly on the stone floor, mingling with the soft trickle of hidden water features. Lily paused before a massive palm, its trunk as thick as her waist, reaching upward toward the distant glass ceiling.

"This one's probably older than both of us combined," she mused, reaching out to touch the rough bark. The texture was alien under her fingertips—fibrous and sturdy.

Devon stood close enough that she could feel his warmth beside her. "Makes you feel small, doesn't it?"

"In the best way," Lily agreed.

A fine mist descended from overhead sprayers, catching the light and transforming into tiny rainbows. Droplets clung to Lily's hair, cool against her scalp. She tilted her face upward, letting the moisture settle on her skin.

Devon laughed beside her, wiping a droplet from his forehead. "Free facial."

They continued along the path, stopping occasionally to read the small placards identifying particularly noteworthy specimens. The humid air made Lily's dress cling to her back, but she didn't mind. There was something freeing about the slight discomfort, a reminder that she was somewhere extraordinary.

"Oh, look at this one," Devon said, pointing to a plant with enormous split leaves. "Monstera deliciosa. Sounds like a villain from a comic book."

Lily giggled. "Monstera deliciosa, the delicious monster. Watch out for her deadly fronds of doom."

"Her arch-nemesis is probably some cactus with an equally ridiculous name," Devon added, his eyes crinkling with amusement.

They turned a corner and discovered a small bench nestled between two towering royal palms, their massive fronds creating a natural canopy overhead. Without discussion, they sat together, their shoulders touching as they took in the scene before them—a miniature waterfall cascading over moss-covered stones into a shallow pool where the water reflected the soaring glass dome above.

"I can see why you come here," Devon said softly. "It feels separate from everything else, like time works differently."

Lily nodded, the constant white noise of the waterfall soothing something deep inside her. "Let's check out the Fern Room next. It's my favorite."

They left the Palm House through a glass doorway that led to a narrow corridor lush with trailing vines and the earthy scent of wet soil. The temperature dropped slightly, the air becoming less tropical but still heavy with moisture.

As they entered the Fern Room, Lily felt a subtle shift in the atmosphere. Unlike the grand cathedral of the Palm House, this space felt intimate, almost secretive. Ferns unfurled in every direction—some delicate and lacy, others massive with prehistoric presence. The ceiling here was lower, creating a sense of being embraced by the verdant growth. Diffused light filtered through the glass, casting everything in a dreamy, ethereal glow.

"This is..." Devon's voice trailed off as he took in the scene.

"I know," Lily whispered, not wanting to disturb the tranquility. "It feels like we've stepped into some fairy tale forest."

They moved deeper into the room, following a winding stone path that curved between ancient-looking ferns. Water trickled somewhere unseen, the gentle sound complementing the hushed quality of the space. Overhead, mist systems activated intermittently, releasing gentle clouds that settled on the plants and visitors alike.

Lily felt Devon's fingers brush against hers, tentative at first. She glanced down as his hand slid into hers, their fingers intertwining with natural ease. The simple connection sent warmth spreading up her arm and into her chest.

"Is this okay?" he asked, his voice soft in the quiet room.

"More than okay," she replied, giving his hand a gentle squeeze.

They continued their exploration hand in hand, no longer concerned about who might see them. Here, surrounded by primeval greenery, such worries seemed insignificant. Devon's thumb traced small circles against her skin as they paused before a massive tree fern, its fronds creating a living umbrella above them.

"These plants have barely changed in millions of years," Lily said, her voice hushed with reverence. "Can you imagine dinosaurs walking through ferns just like these?"

Devon tilted his head, considering. "Makes our problems seem pretty small, doesn't it?"

"Exactly." She leaned closer, her shoulder pressing against his. "That's why I love it here. Perspective."

A small placard caught her attention, and she

tugged Devon toward it. "'Maidenhair fern,'" she read. "'Named for its delicate, hair-like stems.'"

"Beautiful," Devon murmured, but when Lily glanced up, she found him looking at her rather than the fern. Heat rushed to her cheeks under his steady gaze.

They lingered in the Fern Room longer than planned, speaking in hushed tones when they spoke at all. Nearby, a father lifted his small son to touch a high frond while the mother adjusted her daughter's cardigan, whispering something that made the girl giggle. Lily watched the family move as a unit through the mist, their silhouettes merging and separating among the ancient greenery. She felt Devon's fingers tighten around hers as they wound their way through the prehistoric landscape, part of the human parade yet somehow separate in their new intimacy.

"I have one more place to show you," Lily said eventually, leading him toward another doorway. "It's completely different from this."

They stepped through a doorway that transported them from lush humidity into bright, arid heat. The Desert House stretched before them, a startling contrast to the Fern Room's verdant intimacy. Overhead, sunlight poured through the clear glass dome, unfiltered and intense, casting sharp shadows across the sandy terrain.

"Oh," Lily breathed, the word escaping her lips as her eyes adjusted to the brightness.

Devon blinked beside her, his hand still warm in hers. "This is... unexpected."

The landscape before them seemed almost alien—twisted cacti reached toward the ceiling with spiny arms, their silhouettes dramatic against the glass walls. Fat barrel cacti squatted on the sandy floor, their round bodies bristling with needle-sharp spines. In one corner, an enormous agave spread its thick, blue-gray leaves in a perfect rosette, a single towering stalk rising from its center.

"It's like we just crossed continents," Devon said, his voice hushed with wonder. "One minute we're in a prehistoric rainforest, and now..."

"The Sonoran Desert," Lily finished for him, feeling a smile spread across her face as she watched his reaction. The childlike fascination in his expression made something warm unfurl in her chest.

They moved deeper into the space, their footsteps crunching softly on the graveled path. The air was bone-dry here, pulling moisture from Lily's skin, making her lips feel suddenly parched. After the heavy dampness of the previous rooms, the desert's crispness felt almost cleansing.

"Look at these," Devon said, stopping before a collection of small, round cacti that resembled sea urchins. "They're like little green pincushions."

Lily leaned closer, careful not to touch. "Mammillaria, I think. The placard says they bloom with bright pink flowers in spring."

"Hard to imagine anything so prickly producing something delicate."

"That's what makes them special," Lily said, watching as Devon crouched to examine the plants more closely. "Beauty hiding beneath defenses."

A massive saguaro dominated the center of the room, its accordion-pleated trunk rising fifteen feet toward the glass ceiling, arms extending outward like a sentinel guarding the desert. Devon moved toward it, his face tilted upward to take in its full height.

"These can live for two hundred years," he said, reading from the information card. "They don't even grow their first arm until they're seventy-five." He shook his head in amazement. "Imagine living that long and still changing, still growing new parts of yourself."

Lily stepped beside him, close enough that their shoulders touched. "There's something comforting about that, isn't there? The idea that we're never really finished becoming who we are."

Devon turned to look at her, the bright desert light catching the amber flecks in his eyes. "I like that thought."

They wandered through the remainder of the Desert House, admiring the strange beauty of plants that had evolved to survive in the harshest conditions. As they emerged from the conservatory's main entrance, Lily blinked against the fading afternoon light. The day had slipped away while they'd been lost in those verdant worlds.

Devon checked his watch and frowned slightly. "I just realized I've been wearing the same clothes since Thursday morning." He ran a hand down his rumpled shirt. "Would you mind if we stopped somewhere so I could get something fresh to wear?"

"Of course not," Lily said, surprised she hadn't noticed earlier. The thought of him wearing work clothes for nearly three days straight made her smile. "There's a place not far from here—Mike's Menswear. Nothing fancy, but they have decent basics."

"Perfect." Devon's face brightened. "I'm a simple guy. Just need something clean."

They caught the Green Line back toward the Loop, then transferred to a bus that dropped them a block from the store. Mike's Menswear stood wedged between a hardware store and a neighborhood tavern, its faded red awning flapping gently in the late afternoon breeze. The display window featured mannequins dressed in practical attire—sturdy work pants, flannel shirts, and sensible jackets.

A bell jingled as they stepped inside. The store smelled of new denim and cardboard boxes, with fluorescent lights humming overhead. An older man with a measuring tape draped around his neck looked up from behind the counter.

"Help you folks find something?" he called, his voice gruff but friendly.

"Just looking for some basics," Devon replied. "Couple shirts, maybe jeans."

The man nodded toward the back. "Shirts on the left wall, jeans in the center aisle. Dressing room's in the corner if you want to try anything on."

Devon moved through the store with purpose, his fingers sliding along the racks of shirts. He pulled out a simple navy button-down, holding it against his chest.

"What do you think?" he asked, turning to Lily.

She tilted her head, assessing. "The color's good, but..." She reached past him, selecting a slightly different shade—a deep burgundy that caught the warm undertones of his skin. "Try this one instead. It'll complement your complexion better."

Devon raised an eyebrow but took the shirt. "I didn't know you were a fashion consultant."

"Hidden talents," Lily replied with a grin. "I've got opinions about everything."

Lily sat in one of the chairs outside the dressing

rooms, absently flipping through a sports magazine someone had left behind. A middle-aged woman with a short blonde bob stood a few feet away, peering toward the dressing room curtains.

"Frank? How's it look?" the woman called out, shifting her weight from one foot to the other. "Does it fit in the shoulders?"

A muffled grunt came from behind the curtain.

"That's not an answer," the woman sighed, then caught Lily's eye with a look of exasperated solidarity. "Men, right? My husband has absolutely no fashion sense. If I didn't help him, he'd wear the same three shirts until they disintegrated."

Lily laughed, setting down the magazine. "My boyfriend's the same way. He just grabbed the first blue shirt he saw until I stepped in."

The word "boyfriend" tumbled out before she could catch it, hanging in the air between them. Boyfriend. She'd known Devon for barely forty-eight hours, yet the term had slipped out as naturally as breathing. Heat crept up her neck as she realized how right it felt, how easily their connection had slid into something that defied the timeline of their actual acquaintance.

The woman nodded knowingly. "That's why we're here, isn't it? To save them from themselves."

Before Lily could respond, the curtain to Devon's dressing room slid open with a metallic scrape. He stepped out in the burgundy button-down she'd selected, paired with the dark wash jeans. The shirt fit him perfectly, accentuating the breadth of his shoulders while tapering slightly at his waist. The color made his skin glow, just as she'd predicted.

"Well?" he asked, holding his arms out to the sides. "Did you pick a winner?"

Lily took her time looking him up and down, enjoying the way the jeans hugged his thighs, how the shirt made his eyes seem even warmer. "Turn around," she instructed, twirling her finger.

Devon rolled his eyes but complied, rotating slowly to give her the full view. The jeans fit him perfectly from behind too, she noted with appreciation.

"Not bad," she said, deliberately understating her reaction. "Definitely an improvement over what you had on."

Devon caught her gaze, a knowing smile playing at his lips. "Just 'not bad,' huh? You're a tough critic."

"I have standards," she replied primly, but couldn't keep the smile from her face. "The color works on you, though. Really works."

"I'll take that as high praise." Devon looked down at himself, smoothing a hand over the front of the shirt. "It feels good. Better than I expected from a place called Mike's."

The woman with the husband in the other dressing room gave Lily an approving nod. "You've got a good eye," she said. "Your boyfriend looks wonderful in that color. The two of you make quite a striking couple."

Devon's eyebrows shot up, a knowing smile spreading across his face as he caught Lily's gaze. She felt heat rising to her cheeks—boyfriend, that word again, this time echoed back to her by a stranger who'd observed them together for all of five minutes.

"Thank you," Devon said smoothly, his eyes never leaving Lily's face. "But my girlfriend here is the one who makes us both look good. She's got the eye for this sort of thing."

The word "girlfriend" hung in the air between them, deliberate and weighted with meaning. Lily's blush deepened, her heart skipping in her chest. The casual claim of her, the easy way he'd stepped into the role she'd accidentally assigned him—it made something warm unfurl in her stomach.

"Well, she certainly does," the woman agreed, oblivious to the current passing between them. "Frank! Come out and see what this young man is wearing. Maybe you'll be inspired."

Devon stepped closer to Lily, leaning down to whisper near her ear. "Boyfriend, huh?"

"It just slipped out," she murmured, unable to look away from his amused expression.

"I like it," he said simply, his voice low enough that only she could hear. "A lot."

Before she could respond, he straightened and turned back toward the dressing room. "I'm going to try on that other shirt you picked. The gray one."

Lily watched him disappear behind the curtain, her pulse still racing. The ease with which they'd fallen into these roles—boyfriend, girlfriend—should have frightened her. Instead, it felt like slipping into a comfortable sweater she hadn't known was hers.

Twenty minutes later, they stood at the register as the clerk rang up Devon's purchases—the burgundy shirt he wore, plus a gray button-down, two t-shirts, and the dark wash jeans. His old clothes were tucked into one of the store's paper bags, the crisp white with "Mike's Menswear" printed in bold red letters.

"You're sure you want to wear that out?" Lily asked, eyeing the security tag still attached to his sleeve.

"Absolutely," Devon replied as the clerk carefully snipped the plastic tag free. "Feels good to be in something clean."

Outside, the late afternoon sun hung low in the sky, casting long shadows across the sidewalk. Devon looked different in his new clothes—more polished, somehow, though still undeniably himself. He shifted the shopping bag to his left hand, his right finding hers with natural ease.

"Thank you," he said, squeezing her fingers gently. "For today. All of it."

Lily squeezed back, a smile tugging at her lips. "It was my pleasure. Really."

They stood for a moment on the sidewalk, neither seemed inclined to move. The shopping bag rustled between them, a physical reminder of the day they'd shared. Lily felt the weight of possibility suspended in the air—like the moment before rain falls, charged with anticipation.

"I'm starving," Devon said, breaking the spell. "Shopping always makes me hungry."

Lily laughed, the sound light and spontaneous. "We just ate a few hours ago."

"That was breakfast," he pointed out, his eyebrows rising. "It's nearly dinner time now."

She checked her watch, surprised to find he was right. The day had slipped away from them, hours dissolving in each other's company. Her stomach chose that moment to growl, betraying her own hunger.

"Busted," Devon said with a grin. "Your stomach

agrees with me."

"Fine," she conceded. "I could eat. I think we should head back to the Starlight," Lily said, touching the sleeve of Devon's new burgundy shirt. The fabric felt crisp under her fingertips, so different from the well-worn cotton he'd arrived in. "We could get dinner there."

Devon's eyes lit up. "The scene of our first date? Perfect."

First date. The words settled over Lily with surprising weight. Yes, that's what Thursday night had been, though it felt like they'd known each other much longer.

Chapter 10

A Place for Two

The Starlight Diner glowed like a beacon against the darkening sky, its neon sign casting familiar pink and blue shadows across Lily's face as Devon held the door open for her. Less than forty-eight hours ago, she'd been a stranger walking into this same space; now she was something else entirely—something she hadn't quite found the right word for yet.

"After you," Devon said, his voice warm against her ear.

Lily stepped inside, the diner's heat enveloping her like an embrace after the January chill. The scents hit her immediately—sizzling burgers, caramelizing onions, fresh coffee brewing in industrial-sized pots. At the counter, an elderly couple shared a slice of pie, their weathered hands overlapped on the Formica surface. The woman laughed at something her companion said, her head tipping back to reveal a delicate throat that had once been young.

"Some things never change," Devon murmured, his hand finding the small of her back with easy familiarity.

"Table for two?" Gloria appeared at their side, menus tucked under her arm, her familiar face breaking into a smile of recognition. "Well, look who's back. You two are becoming regulars."

Lily felt a flutter in her chest at being recognized, at becoming part of the fabric of this place. "Is our booth open?" she asked, surprising herself with the possessiveness in her voice. Our booth. As if they'd claimed that small corner of the diner as their own after just one visit.

"For you? Always." Gloria winked, leading them toward the same red vinyl booth where they'd shared pancakes and secrets in the early hours of yesterday morning. The tabletop gleamed under the pendant lights, freshly wiped clean, waiting for them.

Devon slid in across from her, the vinyl squeaking beneath him. His new burgundy shirt caught the light, making his brown skin glow warmly against the backdrop of chrome and neon. Lily couldn't help but stare at him, this man who'd somehow become central to her life in less than two days.

"What?" he asked, catching her gaze, a smile playing at the corners of his mouth.

"Nothing," she said, then corrected herself. "Everything. It's just... being back here with you feels different now."

"Good different?"

"Very good different." She reached across the table,

her fingers finding his. The simple contact sent warmth spreading up her arm.

Gloria returned with two waters, the ice clinking against the glass as she set them down. "Know what you want, or do you need a minute?"

Lily hadn't even glanced at the menu. "I'll have a cheeseburger, medium, with fries," she said, the decision requiring no thought. Something about tonight called for comfort food, something substantial and grounding.

"Make that two," Devon added. "And could we get an order of those onion rings too? The ones I saw on that table when we walked in looked amazing."

"You got it, hon. Coming right up." Gloria collected their menus and bustled away, leaving them alone in their small corner of the diner.

Lily watched as Devon's eyes traveled around the space, taking in the chrome fixtures, the neon beer signs, the black and white photographs of old Chicago that lined the walls. His gaze returned to her, softer now.

"I can't believe it was just yesterday morning we were sitting here," he said, his thumb tracing circles on the back of her hand. "Feels like I've known you much longer."

"I was just thinking the same thing." Lily took a sip of her water, the cold shocking against her teeth. "Is that weird? That this feels so... natural?"

"Not weird. Lucky." Devon's smile deepened the creases around his eyes. "Very, very lucky."

The moment was interrupted by a plate of golden onion rings appearing between them, the aroma of fried batter and sweet onion rising in a savory cloud.

"A feast for our eyes and stomachs," Devon said,

plucking an onion ring from the plate and taking a bite. The crisp exterior gave way with a satisfying crunch, revealing the sweet, tender onion inside.

Lily selected one as well, savoring the perfect balance of salt and grease. The familiar comfort of the diner wrapped around her like a cocoon, but everything felt different now. The neon lights that had once seemed harsh now painted Devon's face in a gentle glow, highlighting the warmth in his eyes as he watched her.

"So," Devon said, leaning forward slightly, "we've spent almost forty-eight hours together, and I'm still not tired of you. That's got to be some kind of record."

Lily laughed, the sound bubbling up from somewhere deep inside her. "I was just thinking the same thing. Usually by now I'm making excuses to leave."

"And now?"

"Now I'm trying to think of excuses to stay." She reached for another onion ring, her fingers brushing against his. Even that small contact sent a current of warmth up her arm.

Gloria returned with their burgers, setting the plates down with practiced efficiency. Steam rose from the perfectly grilled patties, the cheese melted just right over the edges. The aroma of beef and salt filled the air between them.

"These look amazing," Devon said, eyeing his burger with appreciation.

"Best in the neighborhood," Gloria replied with a wink before moving on to another table.

Lily picked up her burger, the warmth seeping through the soft bun into her fingertips. She took a bite, closing her eyes as the flavors melded on her tongue — the savory meat, the sharp cheese, the slight tang of the pickle.

When she opened her eyes, Devon was watching her with a soft expression that made her heart flutter.

"What?" she asked, suddenly self-conscious.

"I just like watching you enjoy things," he said simply. "You're fully present in a way most people aren't."

The compliment warmed her more than the food. "It's easier to be present when I'm with you," she admitted. "Everything feels more... real."

Devon nodded, understanding in his eyes. "That's exactly it. Like I've been seeing the world through a filter, and suddenly it's gone."

They ate in comfortable silence for a few moments, the sounds of the diner creating a gentle backdrop — silverware clinking against plates, muted conversations, the hiss of the grill.

"I never expected this," Lily said finally, setting down her burger. "When I walked into The Glass Heel Thursday night, I was just looking for a few hours of escape. Not..." She gestured between them, searching for the right words.

"Not this," Devon finished for her. "Not someone who makes everything feel like home."

Home. The word resonated inside her, striking a chord she hadn't realized was there. Devon did feel like home — not the cavernous Park Ridge home where she'd grown up, but something deeper, more essential. A sense of belonging she'd been chasing all her life.

"You make me feel like I can be myself," she said,

the words coming out in a rush before she could overthink them. "All of myself. Not just the polished parts I show at work, or the careful version I present to strangers. Just... me."

Devon reached across the table, his fingers intertwining with hers. "That's the greatest gift anyone's ever given me, you know. Just being yourself with me."

The sincerity in his voice made her throat tighten. Lily looked down at their joined hands—his broader, with calluses from years of physical work; hers slender, with neatly trimmed nails and softer skin. Different, yet somehow perfectly matched.

"I love you," she said, the words slipping out on an exhale, natural as breathing.

The moment they left her lips, heat rushed to her face. Her eyes widened, shocked at her own boldness. Too soon, far too soon—they'd known each other less than forty-eight hours. She couldn't possibly love him already. Could she?

Devon went still, his expression unreadable for a heartbeat that stretched into eternity. Then his face softened, a smile spreading slowly across his features, crinkling the corners of his eyes. He shifted his hand, placing it gently on top of hers, his palm warm and slightly rough against her skin.

"I love you too, Lily," he said, his voice steady and sure, without a trace of hesitation.

The words hung between them, transforming the air in their small corner of the diner. Lily felt dizzy with the weight of them, with the impossible rightness of this moment.

"Is it crazy?" she whispered, her voice catching. "To feel this way so quickly?"

"Probably," Devon admitted, his thumb tracing circles on the back of her hand. "But I don't care. I've spent my whole life building things—structures, foundations, walls. I know what's solid when I feel it." His eyes held hers, unwavering. "This is solid, Lily."

She nodded, unable to find words that could match the certainty in his voice. Around them, the diner continued its evening rhythm—the sizzle of the grill, the clink of silverware, the murmur of conversations—but it all seemed distant, as if she and Devon existed in a bubble of their own making.

"I've never said that before," she whispered, her voice nearly lost beneath the clatter of dishes and murmur of other diners. She swallowed hard. "Not when I actually meant it."

Devon's expression softened further, a flicker of something like wonder crossing his features. "I'm honored," he said simply. His hand squeezed hers gently. "And I've never meant it more than I do right now."

Gloria dropped the check on the table, and Devon reached for it with a smile. "I've got this one."

"We could split it," Lily offered, but Devon shook his head.

"Not a chance." He slid his credit card into the black folder. "You paid for the conservatory, I pay for dinner. That's how this works."

When Gloria returned with the receipt, Devon signed it with a generous tip. He gathered his shopping bag from Mike's Menswear, the paper crinkling as he hoisted it from beneath the table.

"Ready for the next part of our adventure?" he asked, extending his hand.

Lily's heart fluttered as she slipped her fingers between his. "The Glass Heel," she said, the name carrying new weight now. "Where it all began."

They stepped out into the night, the temperature having dropped while they ate. The sky had deepened to indigo, streetlights casting pools of yellow on the sidewalk. Devon's arm slid around her waist, pulling her close against the chill as they walked the few blocks to the club.

The Glass Heel's crimson sign glowed against the brick façade, casting ruby shadows across the sidewalk. No line had formed yet—it was early, the club just opening for the evening. Lily felt a flutter of nervousness in her stomach. This was different from her solo visit Thursday night. Tonight, she was returning with Devon, entering as a couple rather than a solitary figure seeking temporary escape.

As they approached, Lily spotted Darius's imposing silhouette by the entrance. The head of security stood with his usual calm vigilance, dark eyes scanning the street. When his gaze landed on them, something shifted in his expression—a subtle softening around the eyes, the barest hint of a smile touching his lips.

"Well, look who's back," Darius said, his deep voice carrying easily in the quiet night. "And together this time." His eyes moved between them, taking in their clasped hands, the easy way they leaned toward each other. "You two clean up nice. Make a good-looking pair."

Heat rushed to Lily's cheeks at the simple observation. There was something validating about Darius seeing them as a unit, as if his recognition made their connection more real.

"Thanks, man," Devon said, clasping Darius's

outstretched hand while passing over his ID. The bouncer's handshake was solid, his eyes knowing as he verified Devon's license with a quick, professional scan. Lily slipped her own ID from her wallet, the laminated card cool against her skin. Darius barely glanced at it before handing both back with a subtle nod of approval.

"Echo's been wondering if you'd be back," Darius said, stepping aside to let them pass. "Said she had a feeling about you two."

Warmth greeted them inside the club, along with the familiar scent of perfume, leather, and polished wood. The entrance hall gleamed with subdued elegance, the dark paneling absorbing the low light in a way that made everything feel more intimate. Lily spotted Marisol at the coat check counter, their dark curls framing their heart-shaped face as they sorted through a rack of garments.

When Marisol looked up and saw them, their face lit with a knowing smile. "Well, well," they said, leaning forward on the counter. "Look who found each other after all."

Lily felt heat rise to her cheeks as she slipped off her coat. "Hi, Marisol."

"Honey, you are positively glowing tonight," Marisol said, their gaze moving between Lily and Devon with obvious approval. They took Lily's coat, fingers lingering on the fabric. "And I'm not talking about your highlighter, though that's flawless too. Something's different about you." They leaned closer, voice dropping to a theatrical whisper. "Or should I say someone?"

The blush deepened on Lily's face, spreading down her neck. She couldn't find words to respond, caught between embarrassment and pleasure at being so easily read.

Devon stepped forward, his smile easy and confident. "I've got some things I need to check too," he said, holding up the Mike's Menswear bag. "Mind if I leave this with you?"

"For you? Absolutely." Marisol took the bag with a flourish, their red-painted nails flashing in the low light. "I'll keep it safe and sound right behind the counter." They slipped a numbered tag into Devon's hand, their fingers brushing his. "Don't lose this, handsome."

"Wouldn't dream of it," Devon replied, tucking the tag into his pocket. His hand found the small of Lily's back, warm and steady through the fabric of her dress.

Marisol watched the gesture with undisguised approval. "You two look good together," they said, straightening a row of coat hangers with practiced efficiency. "Like you fit, you know? That's rare in here. Lots of people searching, not so many finding."

"Thank you," Lily managed, finding her voice at last. The simple validation from someone who'd seen countless couples come and go through these doors meant more than she'd expected.

"Echo's at her usual table," Marisol added, gesturing toward the main room. "She mentioned she might want to see you if you came back."

Devon's eyebrows rose slightly. "Is that a good thing or a bad thing?"

Marisol laughed, the sound bright against the club's muted atmosphere. "With Echo? Always a good thing. She doesn't waste time on people who don't interest her."

As they moved away from the coat check, Devon's arm slid around Lily's waist, guiding her toward the main room. The familiar indigo lighting washed over them as they stepped past the velvet curtain, but tonight it felt different—less mysterious, more like coming home.

The Glass Heel hadn't filled yet—just a few early arrivals lounging on velvet couches, nursing first drinks beneath the glow of the dancing lights. A small group chatted near the stage, their laughter soft against the backdrop of DJ Heather's carefully curated mix—her signature blend of house and soul filtering through the expensive sound system at a volume that invited rather than demanded. Two women shared whispered conversations at a corner table, fingers intertwined on the polished surface. The dance floor remained empty beneath the slowly rotating lights, a pristine expanse of possibility waiting for the night to truly begin.

Devon leaned close, his breath warm against her ear. "Let's get a drink."

Lily nodded, suddenly aware of how dry her throat felt. They made their way to the mirrored bar where Julian stood polishing glasses, his movements methodical and precise. His dark curls were pulled back in a low ponytail, revealing the sharp angles of his face. When he looked up and saw them approaching, his expression shifted from professional neutrality to warm recognition.

"Well, look who decided to come back," Julian said, setting down the glass he'd been polishing. "And together this time." His eyes moved between them, taking in their proximity, the easy way Devon's hand rested at Lily's waist.

"Hey, Julian," Devon said, sliding onto a barstool. Lily settled beside him, the leather seat cool against her thighs. "Got any of that honey wheat ale on tap?"

"For you? Always." Julian reached for a glass, his movements smooth and practiced. "And for the lady?"

He turned to Lily, one eyebrow raised in question.

"Strawberry daiquiri, please," she said, surprising herself with the choice. She usually opted for wine, something restrained and predictable, but tonight felt different. Tonight called for something sweet and vibrant, something that matched the fizzy feeling in her chest.

Julian's mouth quirked into a knowing smile. "Going tropical on me, huh? Must be something in the air." He began gathering ingredients, his hands moving with fluid grace. "Or someone." His gaze flicked meaningfully toward Devon.

Heat rushed to Lily's cheeks. "It just sounded good," she mumbled, though she couldn't keep the smile from her lips.

"Uh-huh." Julian's tone was playful as he poured rum into a shaker. "And I'm sure it has nothing to do with the fact that you two can't stop looking at each other like you've discovered a new continent."

Devon laughed, the sound warm and unembrrassed. "Is it that obvious?"

"Only to everyone with eyes," Julian replied, his teasing gentle. He placed Devon's beer on the bar, the amber liquid catching the indigo light. "But it looks good on you both."

Miko gave them a subtle nod of recognition, her dark eyes lingering on their joined hands for a moment before she returned to her work, a ghost of a smile on her lips.

Lily's gaze drifted past Miko to the corner of the bar, where a familiar figure sat watching the room with quiet intensity. Echo Dela Cruz occupied her usual spot, a jewel-toned dress draping elegantly over her statuesque frame, her raven-black hair styled in perfect vintage rolls. Even in the club's subdued lighting, her silver-gray eyes seemed to gleam as they settled on Lily and Devon.

As if sensing their attention, Echo rose from her seat with fluid grace. She moved through the early crowd with deliberate steps, her presence commanding the space without effort. The club's indigo lighting caught the subtle shimmer of her dress as she approached, transforming ordinary movement into something almost ethereal.

"Lily Warren," Echo said, her low, musical voice somehow carrying perfectly despite the background music. "And Devon Carter. Together, as it should be." She extended her hand to Lily first, her touch cool and gentle. "Welcome back to The Glass Heel."

"Thank you," Lily managed, suddenly feeling both nervous and honored by Echo's personal greeting. There was something in the club owner's gaze—a knowing depth that made Lily feel seen in ways that went beyond the physical.

Echo turned to Devon, clasping his hand between both of hers. "I had a feeling about you two," she said, her voice warm with quiet certainty. "Some connections are written in starlight long before they manifest."

Devon's hand found the small of Lily's back, a gentle pressure that steadied her. "It feels that way," he agreed, his voice carrying a conviction that made Lily's heart flutter.

Echo's silver eyes moved between them, taking in details with an attentiveness that felt almost mystical. "The energy between you has shifted," she observed. "Deepened. It suits you both."

Lily felt heat rise to her cheeks at the intimate

assessment. Echo spoke as if she could see the invisible threads that had woven her and Devon together over the past forty-eight hours—the confessions, the vulnerability, the words of love exchanged over diner burgers.

"I hope you'll make yourselves at home tonight," Echo continued, gesturing toward the club with an elegant sweep of her hand. "The Glass Heel has a way of revealing what we need most, even when we don't recognize it ourselves."

The club's entrance curtain parted, drawing Echo's attention. Two women stepped into the main room—one with black curls falling in soft waves down her back, the other with wavy chestnut hair just past her shoulders. Echo's expression softened with recognition.

"If you'll excuse me," she said, her voice warm with affection. "Elena and Claire have arrived, and I've been expecting them." She touched Lily's shoulder lightly. "We'll speak again before the night ends."

With that, Echo glided away, leaving them at the bar with their drinks. Julian leaned forward, his forearms resting on the polished surface, eyes bright with undisguised curiosity.

"So," he said, drawing out the word as he slid a napkin beneath Lily's daiquiri. "Are we going to talk about the fact that you two vanished after Thursday night and reappeared looking like..." He gestured between them, searching for the right words. "This?"

Lily felt heat bloom across her cheeks. She took a quick sip of her daiquiri, the sweet-tart flavor dancing on her tongue as she tried to formulate a response that wouldn't reveal just how much had happened between them.

Devon chuckled beside her, his shoulder pressing warmly against hers. "Like what, exactly?"

Julian rolled his eyes. "Like you've been living in each other's pockets for days. Like you've known each other for years instead of—what was it? Forty-eight hours?" He reached for another glass to polish, though his gaze never left them. "Come on, I need details. You can't expect me to serve you drinks without getting the full story."

"We just..." Lily began, then faltered. How could she possibly condense everything they'd shared into casual bar conversation? The diner at dawn, falling asleep in each other's arms, the conservatory, the words exchanged over burgers. It felt too precious, too intimate to reduce to anecdotes.

"We connected," Devon finished simply, his fingers finding hers beneath the bar.

Julian snorted. "Yeah, I can see that. But what happened after you left here? Where did you go? What did you do? I'm dying over here."

Miko appeared at Julian's side, setting down a tray of clean glasses. Though her expression remained neutral, Lily noticed how she slowed her movements, clearly interested in their response despite her apparent focus on arranging the glassware.

"We went to the Starlight Diner," Lily admitted, the memory warming her from within. "Talked until sunrise."

"The Starlight?" Julian's eyebrows arched knowingly. "That place has witnessed more first dates from this bar than I can count." He polished a glass with practiced efficiency, a smile playing at his lips. "Something about those vinyl booths just makes people honest."

"There's a kind of magic there," Devon said, his thumb tracing circles on the back of Lily's hand. "Like the rest of the world just falls away."

Julian leaned closer, voice dropping conspiratorially. "And after the diner? I'm guessing you didn't just shake hands and go your separate ways."

Lily took another sip of her daiquiri, using the moment to gather herself. "We went back to my place," she said finally.

Julian's eyes widened with delight. "Now we're getting somewhere! And?"

"And we talked more," Devon said, amusement coloring his voice. "Got to know each other."

"'Talked,'" Julian repeated, making air quotes with his fingers. "Right," Julian said with a smirk. "Because that's all people do when they disappear together for two days." He leaned forward on his elbows, eyes bright with curiosity. "Come on, I need more than that. What happened after the diner? Did you sleep at all? Did you leave the apartment?"

Lily felt her cheeks warm as Devon's hand squeezed hers under the bar. She glanced at him, finding his expression amused rather than uncomfortable.

"We went to the Garfield Park Conservatory today," Devon offered, taking a sip of his beer.

Julian's eyebrows shot up. "The conservatory? That's... surprisingly wholesome."

"What were you expecting?" Lily asked, unable to keep the smile from her voice.

"I don't know. Maybe a whirlwind trip to Vegas? Secret tattoos with each other's names?" Julian shrugged, his dark curls bouncing with the movement. "The way you two are looking at each other, I half expected you to walk in here engaged."

Miko appeared at Julian's side, ostensibly to retrieve a bottle of top-shelf vodka, but Lily noticed how her movements slowed, her attention clearly caught by their conversation despite her neutral expression.

"No rings yet," Devon said with a laugh that vibrated through Lily's chest. "Just pancakes, plants, and..." He paused, his eyes meeting Lily's with a warmth that made her stomach flutter. "Connections."

Julian groaned dramatically. "You're killing me with the vague answers. I need specifics. Did you go anywhere else? Meet the parents? Adopt a puppy together?"

"I already have a dog," Lily said. "Poppy. She's a Papillon."

"And she likes me," Devon added with a hint of pride.

"The dog approves? That's serious," Julian said, pointing at them with the bar towel. "Animals know things."

Miko's lips curved into the ghost of a smile as she mixed a martini with practiced precision, her eyes occasionally flicking toward their conversation.

"What about you, Julian?" Devon asked, smoothly deflecting. "How's your week been?"

"Oh no, we're not doing that." Julian wagged a finger between them. "You don't get to change the subject. I want to know how you went from strangers to..." He gestured at their obvious closeness. "This. In two days."

Lily took another sip of her daiquiri, the sweet-tart flavor dancing on her tongue. "Sometimes you just know," she said softly, surprising herself with the admission.

Julian's teasing expression softened. "Yeah? And what exactly do you know?"

Devon's thumb traced gentle circles on the back of Lily's hand. "That some connections don't need time to be real," he said, his voice low but certain.

Miko sidled closer, pretending to restock the glassware while clearly eavesdropping. Her practiced movements couldn't quite hide her interest as Julian leaned across the bar, eyes bright with curiosity.

"So wait—after the diner you went straight to your place? And you've been there the whole time?" Julian pressed, mixing a mojito for another patron without taking his eyes off them. "Two days together and you're already looking at each other like that?"

Lily felt her cheeks flush. "Not the whole time. We did eventually leave the apartment."

"Only because we ran out of food," Devon added with a grin that made Lily's stomach flutter.

Julian nearly dropped the bottle he was holding. "Oh my god, you two are killing me. I need details! What exactly happened at your place? And don't say 'we talked' again because nobody looks this happy after just talking."

"Some things are private, Julian," Lily said, but couldn't keep the smile from her face.

"Private is code for scandalous," Julian said with a wink. "Come on, at least tell me if it was good."

"Julian!" Lily squeaked, mortified.

Devon laughed, his arm sliding around her waist. "Let's just say we discovered we have excellent... chemistry."

Julian's eyebrows shot up. "Chemistry, huh? Is that what the kids are calling it these days?"

Miko's lips twitched in a barely-there smile as she slid a freshly mixed cocktail toward a waiting customer. Though she maintained her composed exterior, her eyes kept drifting back to their conversation.

"And the conservatory? Whose idea was that?" Julian continued, undeterred. "Sounds suspiciously like a real date."

"Mine," Lily admitted. "I wanted to show him something beautiful."

"So you've met her dog, seen her plants... what's next? Moving in together?"

Devon chuckled. "We're taking things one day at a time."

"One very intense day at a time, from the looks of it," Julian observed, glancing between them. "I've seen people date for months who don't look at each other the way you two do."

Lily took another sip of her daiquiri, feeling the sweet burn of rum warm her throat. The club had begun to fill around them, the early trickle of patrons becoming a steady stream. The dance floor no longer stood empty—a handful of couples had claimed the space, moving together beneath the indigo lights.

Devon's gaze followed hers, taking in the growing crowd and the pulsing rhythm that seemed to vibrate through the floorboards. He turned back to her, his eyes warm with invitation.

"Want to dance?" he asked, setting his beer down on the bar. "Might be our only escape from the interrogation."

Julian clutched his chest in mock offense. "I'm just showing interest in your happiness!"

Lily laughed, taking his hand. "Lead the way."

Devon guided her to the dance floor, his fingers interlaced with hers, the warmth of his palm a constant reminder of their connection. As they reached the center of the floor, the music shifted—something slower, with a pulsing bass that seemed to match the rhythm of Lily's heartbeat. Devon turned to face her, his eyes reflecting the indigo lights above them.

Unlike Thursday night, there was no hesitation, no careful distance maintained. Devon's arms encircled her waist with confident familiarity, drawing her against him until she could feel the solid warmth of his chest. Lily's hands found their way to his shoulders, then slid behind his neck, her fingers reaching the edge of his afro where the tight coils felt like velvet against her fingertips.

They moved together with a synchronicity that took her breath away. Her body remembered his, knew how to match his movements, how to follow his lead without thought. His burgundy shirt felt smooth beneath her fingertips, the fabric warming with their shared heat.

"No more strangers," Devon murmured against her ear, his breath sending shivers down her spine.

"No more strangers," she agreed, letting her cheek rest against his shoulder.

The dance floor filled around them, bodies moving in the indigo glow, but Lily barely noticed. The world had narrowed to this—Devon's arms around her waist, his heartbeat against her chest, the subtle scent of his cologne mingling with the fabric softener from his new shirt. They swayed together, sometimes talking in soft murmurs, sometimes silent, content in the simple pleasure of touch.

Occasionally, Lily caught glimpses of Echo at her usual table, her silver-gray eyes observing them with quiet interest. Unlike Thursday night, when Echo's attention had felt mysterious, almost mystical, tonight it felt like recognition—as if the club owner was witnessing something she'd anticipated all along.

The music shifted again, the tempo increasing. Devon spun her outward, then back into his arms with a fluid grace that made her laugh with delight. His hands found her hips, guiding her movements as they fell into the faster rhythm. Lily let herself go, surrendering to the music and to him, her body moving with a freedom she rarely allowed herself.

Time seemed to fold in on itself, minutes blurring into hours as they alternated between dancing and brief returns to the bar for water or rest. Julian continued his good-natured teasing whenever they approached, while Miko served their drinks with knowing smiles that grew less subtle as the night progressed.

"You two are making everyone else look bad," Julian commented during one of their breaks, sliding fresh waters across the bar. "Even the regulars are watching you."

Lily glanced around, suddenly aware of the appreciative glances directed their way. The realization should have made her self-conscious, but with Devon's arm around her waist, she found she didn't mind being seen—being recognized as part of something beautiful.

They returned to the dance floor, hands entwined, finding their rhythm together beneath the indigo lights.

The club had reached its peak now, bodies moving in synchronized chaos, the air thick with perfume and cologne and the electric charge of possibilities.

As the night deepened, Lily noticed the crowd beginning to thin. Couples departed arm in arm, lone dancers gathered their belongings, the energy of the room shifting from frenzied celebration to something quieter, more intimate. The DJ transitioned to mellower tracks, a signal that the night was winding down.

"Should we head out?" Devon asked, his lips close to her ear to be heard above the music. His hand rested warm against the small of her back, his body still swaying gently with hers to the fading beat.

Lily nodded, suddenly aware of the pleasant ache in her feet from hours of dancing. "Let's get our things from Marisol."

They made their way through the thinning crowd, nodding goodbyes to faces that had become familiar over the course of the evening. Lily felt a curious mixture of satisfaction and reluctance—happy to have shared this night with Devon, yet somehow not ready for it to end, despite knowing they'd be leaving together.

As they approached the coat check, Lily spotted Marisol's dark curls behind the counter. Before they could reach it, however, a figure stepped into their path, her jewel-toned dress catching the low light in shimmering waves.

Echo stood before them, silver-gray eyes luminous in the club's fading glow. Her presence seemed to create a pocket of stillness around them, as if the music had dimmed just for this moment.

"I've been watching you two all night," Echo said, her melodic voice carrying easily despite the background noise. "The way you move together, the energy between you—it's transformed since Thursday." Her gaze moved between them, seeing something beyond the physical. "What was potential has become kinetic."

Lily felt Devon's hand tighten slightly around hers, a silent acknowledgment of Echo's perceptiveness.

"The Glass Heel recognizes its own," Echo continued, her lips curving into a gentle smile. "And you both belong here now, in ways you didn't before." She paused, her silver eyes settling on Lily with quiet intensity. "I believe you're ready for the Heel's Nest."

The words hung in the air between them. Lily felt her heartbeat quicken, remembering the whispers she'd heard about the exclusive boutique hotel above the club—the uniquely themed rooms, each designed for exploration and intimacy, offered only to Echo's most trusted guests.

"The Nest?" Devon's voice held a note of surprise. "We'd be honored."

Echo reached into a hidden pocket of her dress and withdrew a brass key attached to a heavy crimson tassel. The number 207 was etched into its surface, the digits gleaming in the low light. She held it out to Devon, who accepted it with visible surprise.

"Room 207," Echo said, her voice melodic and low. "The Blush Desire."

Lily's heart quickened, her pulse a rapid flutter beneath her skin. The Heel's Nest was legendary among Glass Heel regulars—whispered about but rarely seen, an invitation-only sanctuary above the club where couples could explore their deepest desires.

"What will we find there?" Lily asked, her voice barely above a whisper.

Echo's silver-gray eyes caught the indigo light, transforming them into something otherworldly. Her lips curved into that familiar enigmatic smile that seemed to hold secrets of the universe.

"Everyone discovers something different about the room," she replied, her voice like velvet against Lily's ears. "And about themselves. The space merely offers possibility—what you find there depends entirely on what you bring with you." Her gaze moved between them, seeing far more than their physical forms. "Some find pleasure, others find truth," Echo continued, her fingers releasing the key into Devon's palm. "The room becomes what you need it to be."

The brass felt warm against Devon's skin as he closed his fingers around it. Lily watched the exchange, a shiver of anticipation traveling up her spine.

"Is it..." Lily hesitated, searching for the right words. "Is it already prepared for us?"

Echo's laugh was like wind chimes in a gentle breeze. "The Blush Desire is always ready. It exists in a perpetual state of welcome." With a graceful turn of her wrist, Echo indicated a velvet-roped area tucked into the shadows beyond the main floor. "The stairs in the VIP section will take you directly to the second floor. No need to check in or sign anything. The room is yours until morning."

Devon slipped the key into his pocket, the weight of it somehow significant against his thigh. He met Lily's eyes, a smile playing at the corners of his mouth. "Thank you, Echo. This is unexpected but... wonderful."

Echo stepped back, her silver-gray eyes lingering on them with quiet satisfaction. "The night has more to offer you both. Enjoy discovering what that might be." With a graceful nod, she turned and glided back toward her corner table, leaving them standing together at the edge of the thinning crowd.

Lily's heart thundered against her ribs as Devon's fingers found hers, warm and solid. The invitation to the Heel's Nest hung between them, charged with possibility.

www.ingramcontent.com/pod-product-compliance
Lightning Source LLC
Chambersburg PA
CBHW031047160726
47991CB00005B/2052